THE IDES OF APRIL

THE·IDES OF·APRIL

MARY·RAY

BETHLEHEM BOOKS • IGNATIUS PRESS
BATHGATE, N.D.   SAN FRANCISCO

©1974, 1999 Mary Ray
This edition slightly revised by the author

Cover illustration ©1999 Gino d'Achille

Cover design by Davin Carlson

First Bethlehem Books edition, April 1999

ISBN 978–1–883937–43–0
Library of Congress catalog card number: 98–83214

Bethlehem Books • Ignatius Press
10194 Garfield Street South
Bathgate, ND 58216
www.bethlehembooks.com

Printed in the United States on acid free paper

THE IDES OF APRIL

CONTENTS

ROME, A.D. 62

DRAMATIS PERSONÆ

Patricians

CAIUS POMPONIUS AFER	Senator
DOMINA FAUSTINA	His stepmother
DECIANUS GALLUS	His stepbrother
DOMINA BLANDINA	His daughter
CAMILLUS RUFUS	A military tribune
GALERIUS	Camillus's friend

People of Rome

MACROBIUS	A prison governor
VARRO	A market porter
MATIDIA	His aunt
FIGULUS	A barber
VIBULANUS	A butcher

The household of Caius Pomponius

ASSINIUS	The steward
HYLAS	The senator's secretary
NISSA	Hylas's mother, Domina Faustina's maid

MEROPE | Now Domina Blandina's maid
AULUS | The senator's valet

DIONYSIOS | Secretary for Correspondence from the Eastern Provinces in the Imperial Household

All these people are imaginary, but Thrasea Paetus, senator and former consul, is not. During his lifetime Rome was ruled by three emperors, Gaius Caligula, Claudius, and Nero. Caligula succeeded Tiberius in A.D. 37 and was murdered in A.D. 41. Then Claudius, his uncle, became Emperor. When he died in A.D. 54, his successor was Nero, who married the daughter of Claudius, Octavia. In A.D. 62, Nero was twenty-five years old.

THE IDES OF APRIL

I

THE COPPERSMITHS' STREET

HYLAS THE SECRETARY found the young man he was looking for in the entrance hall of the Baths of Agrippa, talking with a group of friends. Hylas was in no hurry; it was a treat to be away from his desk in his master's library for an hour, alone in the afternoon. Besides, there were few people in Rome he admired as much as Camillus Rufus, so he was content to wait for him. He moved around so that there would be some hope of catching the young tribune's eye when the conversation finished, and stood quietly as he had been taught, not lounging against a pillar or pushing himself forward. Hylas had been born a slave, he was seventeen years old, and he knew how to behave.

Camillus was enjoying himself. It was the first day of the Festival of Ceres and he had spent the morning at the Circus watching the races. He was home on leave for the first time from his legion in Germany, and was savoring the delightful experience of being suddenly grown up. Now he could talk easily to the group of men whom he used to think of as friends of his father, the people one called sir, who asked you questions about school. It was amazing the difference that one winter in Germany as a junior staff officer had made. Even his toga felt light and unfamiliar since he had learned to ignore the weight of a breastplate. And then there had been the most important happening of his leave, his marriage to the younger sister of his best friend. He had been nervous about it even though it had been arranged years ago and he had known Blandina by sight since she was a child. In the days since then he had discovered that she could be an amusing companion; he would be sorry to leave her behind when he went north again.

Hylas knew all about the marriage, being a member of the household of the senator Caius Pomponius Afer, who was the father of Domina Blandina, the bride. And it was Blandina who had sent him to find her husband.

"But, Galerius," Camillus was saying to the friend who was standing with a hand on his shoulder, "the balance of that statue is all wrong. No discus thrower ever had all the weight on the left foot so late in the throw. Look, he's already shifted the discus into his right hand." He shrugged off the restraining hand so that he could demonstrate what he meant.

Galerius, who looked languid compared to his shorter, more enthusiastic friend, said, "My dear Camillus, pity the poor model. No one could keep that halfway position properly for more than a few minutes. He had to shift forward and the sculptor could only copy what he saw."

"Then he shouldn't have tried to do that pose at all, if he couldn't get it right. A Greek wouldn't have done it. That sculptor must have been a Syrian or something. Surely I'm right, Senator?" He turned to a thin, gray-haired man who had been watching his enthusiasm with quiet amusement.

"Camillus, you know far more about athletics than I ever did, even at your age; don't expect an opinion from me.

The statue lacks something, I admit, and I am prepared to believe that it is because the athlete is standing incorrectly if you say so. And that reminds me: my old friend Catonius Justus, who is president of the Games of Ceres, has invited me to share the spectacle from his box on one day during the festival. Now I can think of few ways of spending a day that would give me less pleasure, but there are some invitations that are impossible to refuse. Would it amuse you to come with me?"

Camillus's face glowed, and it was clear that young Galerius would have given a lot to be included in an invitation to watch the races from the best box in the Circus. "What a finish to my leave! Thrasea Paetus, you are really too good to me!"

"Hardly. But I was secretly hoping that your expertise would cover my ignorance. I used to bring home toys for you from the East when your father and I were stationed together in Bithynia. I am delighted to see that in spite of your new military swagger you are not too old for treats! I will send you word, then."

As he left, the group parted politely, for Thrasea Paetus was a former consul and one of the most respected men in the city. That gave Hylas his chance and he managed to attract the young tribune's attention. Camillus recognized him at once; Hylas had often attended Marcus, his master's son, during the last summer before they went north to begin their military service. Hylas was probably better educated than Marcus, for Caius Pomponius had recognized that the child born to his mother's maid was unusually intelligent and had paid for him to go to school. Camillus was fond of his friend, but Marcus knew more about the form of the chariot teams in the Circus than about the works of Vergilius. Camillus prided himself on appreciating both, but could never have guessed that that was partly why Hylas admired him so much.

"You wanted me?" he asked.

"Yes, noble Tribune, Domina Blandina sent me. She is at the Villa Pomponia and hoped that it would be possible for you to meet her there."

"What's that, an invitation to dinner, or is your wife afraid to come home in the dark?" said Galerius, laughing.

"When you are married, my friend, you will understand these matters better! I'm leaving Rome in ten days' time, and there are still arrangements to be made about Blandina. I'll see you tomorrow at the usual place?"

Hylas followed him out through the pillared portico into the brilliant spring sunshine in the small square opposite the Theater of Pompey. "You're going back to the villa, then? I'll walk with you. There's so much rebuilding going on that I'm out of date already. I expect you know the quickest ways. Next time my wife sends for me from half across the city she'll have to send a litter!"

Hylas, two paces behind, flushed pink with pleasure and wished that all the members of his master's family were as polite. Domina Blandina for one had been imperious from the age of two, when her tempers had shaken the whole house. She was fifteen now and had changed very little, but perhaps Camillus would not need to discover that yet.

Camillus led the way at a good pace through the holiday crowds, past the Circus Flaminius and the Forum of Julius. It was the hour in the afternoon when, with the shops shut for the beginning of the festival and all public business suspended, people came out to walk up and down and enjoy the air. There had been a thunderstorm the night before and the morning had started cloudy, but now it was warm and the shadows lay dark and sharp across the worn paving stones, except where the swallows gathering along the cornices of the temples flickered and swooped after gnats.

The cripples were out as well, hoping for good pickings from the superstitious or the generous. Withered legs trailed awkwardly across the pavements, and misshapen children caught at passing togas. Hylas turned his head away from one unpleasant sight. He had no money to give, slaves never had, for they must save like squirrels in autumn against the hope of buying their freedom. The crowds were good-tempered enough, but the city guard was already out in force, expecting trouble later. Rome was never an easy city; these days it was an ant heap of underworked and underfed freedmen squashed into squalid rooms in rickety blocks of flats. And then there were the slaves, better fed, some not overworked except when they were hired out to do the tasks that free men disdained. But never free, never unhurried, never able to stop to listen to the man who was making a speech from the public rostrum over there without having to account for the time later. No, never free to choose something as simple as that.

Hylas pulled himself together to see that Camillus had got ahead of him in the crowd and had stopped to wait. "Where now?" he asked. "We don't need to go all the way around by the Via Tusculana, do we?"

"No, my lord, we can go up the Coppersmiths' Street and cut off a corner."

Hylas went ahead. The narrow, muddy alleys they were now in looked strange with the shutters up outside the shops and the usual festoons of cooking pots and sandals locked away, but they were still crowded with people making their way down to the more spacious squares and colonnades in the center of the city. It was too noisy to talk, and they had to pick their way among the mounds of rubble and stacks of timber being used by the builders of a new block of flats. There were men working there even during the holidays. The walls were already four stories high and the wooden scaffolding looked frail as a vine climbing up the side of the unplastered walls.

They stopped for two slaves hauling on a pulley to raise a load of bricks up to the level where the men were working. Hylas followed the swaying bundle with his eyes as it spun on the rope. A corner caught against the jutting end of a ladder at the level of the third floor and the men below gave the rope a sharp tug to free it. The bricks swung out, but as they jerked upward they struck the ladder a heavier blow, like a battering ram gathering force.

Camillus was looking at the men below, cursing them mildly because he wanted to pass, but Hylas saw the ladder begin to slide even before the man who had been climbing it screamed as he lost his footing. Camillus, caught off balance, stumbled against the opposite wall as Hylas knocked him to one side.

The man fell screaming in a long wail like a dog at midnight, to land with an ugly thud across a pile of bricks below. Then came the ladder, banging against the scaffolding poles and shaking down loose mortar and wood. The whole fragile framework shook and the men high above cried out and clung to the unfinished wall.

Camillus pulled Hylas back beside him into cover until the last of the bricks had fallen and it seemed that the rest of the scaffold would not collapse at once. One of the men below had a cut head, and they could hear the foreman bellowing above like a startled bull. The slave who had fallen still lay across the scattered bricks. Hylas took one step forward but Camillus held him back.

"No, don't you see how he's lying? He broke both his back and his neck by the look of it."

Hylas was glad that the body lay with its face turned away, but red was already oozing down over the bricks. An overseer had reeled out of the wineshop down the street; he tested the scaffolding and shouted up angrily at the men above, who were still frozen motionless, afraid to move.

"Go on, what are you waiting for? It's safe enough."

There were sounds of work starting again and someone threw a sack over the body. One of the two men who had been on the rope was standing looking at it with his hands hanging loose at his sides and his face sick.

Camillus noticed the face, too. "Come on," he said to Hylas. "I don't expect you enjoy seeing slaves beaten, and he'll be wishing he could change places with his dead mate before the overseer's finished."

Hylas hurried after him, feeling sick and cold. He had seen men die before—in the streets, in the Circus, criminals dragged to execution; what small child in Rome had not? But he was a Greek, and did not think that violent and messy death was an entertainment. Camillus stopped at the top of the hill and turned back to Hylas. He seemed quite unruffled, until the slave noticed that there was sweat on his forehead, and though the afternoon was fine it was not warm enough for that.

"Thank you," he said. "I would not have liked to break my neck that way. Death by falling slave is not something I had thought of before." Then he grinned at Hylas, seeing him embarrassed. "No, I'm not going to give you money, I should insult you with a small coin, and to tell the truth, I haven't enough with me to reward you properly. I never take money out on a holiday, I might spend it."

Hylas went pink for the second time that afternoon, and ducked his head, and Camillus touched him lightly on the shoulder. "I might be able to help you sometime with something more practical than a silver coin. Ask me if I can, if I'm here. That's not much of a promise, but who knows what god is listening? Now where are we? Oh, I see, the turning's just up there on the left, isn't it?"

Again he went on ahead, and Hylas followed him to the gates of his master's house, wondering what made men so different and gave some the light touch of an artist on a stringed instrument in their dealings with people, and others the consideration of a drunken man blundering in the dark.

II

CAIUS POMPONIUS

THE STREETS THAT wound across the shallow slopes of the Caelian Hill were narrow, with many high blank walls and dark gateways. It was hard to tell if they concealed a warehouse or the villa of a patrician household, secure from the noise and dirt of pack animals passing to the new great market. Hylas, when he had left the Villa Pomponia an hour before, had dropped the problems of the family as one drops a heavy cloak on the floor. As Camillus knocked on the double gates, the weight of them came down on him again.

Usually he did not think too much about the life of the family who owned him, as a child does not think about his own parents. Masters, like fathers, are there and nearly impossible to alter. But now something was wrong, and if he had known what it was, Hylas would have felt easier. No one had quarreled audibly in the small rooms around the double courtyards of the house. Hylas knew that his master was not short of money. He had just married his daughter successfully, and his son was giving satisfaction. Also, no one seemed to be ill. Life seemed normal, as normal as it must appear to farmers picking olives on the slopes of a sleeping volcano. So why was Caius Pomponius, the red-faced and affable, suddenly quiet and at home every evening?

9

The porter opened the gates and Camillus led the way into the atrium. Hylas followed him past the fish tank in the middle and under the pillared entrance to the peristyle at the back where the family usually gathered. They were all there. Blandina, his young mistress, small and slightly plump, sitting with her grandmother, Domina Faustina, in the warm corner that caught the late afternoon sun; Caius Pomponius, Faustina's stepson, talking to the son of her first marriage, Decianus Gallus.

Blandina was playing with a small pet monkey, a tiny thing with a face like an old man's and a thin gold chain fastened to the red leather collar around its neck. "Camillus," she greeted her husband with delight, "now please agree with me. Father is suggesting I go with the family to the villa at Nomentum for the summer as I always have. I don't really have to go with your great-aunt to Misenum? It's so hot there!"

Hylas paused in the doorway of his master's library on the other side of the courtyard to see what would happen. Blandina was used to getting her own way.

Camillus greeted the rest of the family and then sat down on the marble bench near his wife's chair. "Aunt Marcella would be very disappointed. She's having the villa reopened especially and I think her steward has gone down already to supervise what needs doing."

"Then of course, my dear Camillus, there's nothing more to be said. Blandina could perhaps come to us in the autumn for a few days. Nomentum is delightful during the vintage, and there's no hope of your being home by then," said Caius Pomponius.

Blandina loosed the gold chain, so that the monkey ran across to Camillus and climbed onto his shoulder. She was still smiling sweetly, but her eyes were very bright and dark.

"Go on then, Scipio, pull his hair. Misenum may be smart, but I hate the sea!"

"Blandina, if Domina Marcella has already gone to trouble and expense on your behalf, then that should be enough for you. Your duty is to your husband's family now."

Domina Faustina had a quiet, flat voice, but it ended most arguments, and Blandina recognized this even now when she was supposed to be grown up. The woman she had always thought of as her grandmother was the real ruler of the household and always had been, the one unchanging rock when Blandina's father was away after his wife had died. She was a small, solid woman with a heavy face and gray hair piled always, in the intricate fashion of an older generation, around a silver crown. Hylas knew her to be firm, usually just, but cold. She never raised her voice, because it never occurred to her that anyone would challenge her authority, and on the rare occasions when they did, she overwhelmed them as effortlessly as a flow of lava engulfs an olive tree.

Her other son, Decianus, had been standing behind his mother's chair. He was younger than his stepbrother, a thin man with a long face and bony neck who seemed colorless when he was near his mother; away from her, he had a biting tongue. Caius Pomponius had always seemed to dislike him, but during the last month they had been together at the Villa Pomponia more than usual. Yes, that was one change that was not easy to account for, unless they had made up the coolness which dated from the time when Caius had opposed Decianus's motion in the Senate the year before.

Blandina, who had got up after her grandmother spoke to her, was drifting about the peristyle, pausing to tweak a spray of flowers from the pink oleander and crush the petals between her fingers. She disappeared for a moment between the pillars at the far end, and then Hylas, turning from the library door to hang up his cloak, was surprised to find her on the threshold. She seemed as startled to see him.

"Oh, you're here. Hylas, I . . ."

Camillus, trying to disentangle the monkey from his hair, appeared behind her. "Blandina, we must go. I'll call for your litter; we mustn't be late for dinner. Oh, I must tell you, this afternoon when we were in the Coppersmiths' Street Hylas saved my life."

But Blandina had already gone, with a swirl of her embroidered tunic and a sharp look of dislike at Hylas. Camillus grinned and shrugged his shoulders, which made the monkey cling on tighter.

"Ooch! Hylas, come and save my life again." The slave loosed the clinging fingers from the thick brown hair, cropped close to fit under a helmet, and took the little creature out to Merope, Blandina's maid, a short dark girl with Egyptian eyes who had come from the household of Pomponius. There was a small bustle of parting. Blandina had already gone through to the atrium, but before her husband could join her she appeared again between the dark pillars.

"Camillus, you were in a hurry and now I'm waiting. Look, I've even made my offering at the family shrine!"

Camillus followed her into the outer courtyard, where the tall wooden cupboard that housed the family gods stood against the eastern wall with its small table for offerings before it. Blandina had partly opened one of the doors and put the bunch of violets that had been pinned to the neck of her tunic on the table.

"There, I wanted to see if the tiny terra-cotta Hestia was still there. No one ever dusts her now I'm married."

Camillus looked suddenly uneasy. Perhaps Blandina was being edgy because she was not pleased at losing an argument, but he had been hoping that the way she had taken his first disagreement was an omen for the future. At least she had not really complained. The litter was waiting and the porter closed the gates behind them.

The sun dipped down behind the high roofs that crowded above the villa, and the peristyle seemed colder and full of shadows. Above, on the far side, where the grandfather of the present master had laid out a garden, there was now the solid bulk of an insula, a block of flats six stories high, with the balconies on the fifth and sixth floors looking straight down into the courtyards of the villa. Building land in the city was scarce now, and old Quintus, Caius's father, had paid off some awkward political debts with what he had got from that sale.

Hylas went back to the quiet of his library. He had work to finish that his master would expect to find ready next day, holiday or no holiday. Decianus Gallus was still talking to his mother in the peristyle; it looked as if he was staying to dinner.

As Hylas unrolled and weighted down the scroll onto which he was copying the household's corrected accounts, he wondered what Blandina had wanted in the library. He had never seen her read a book in her life; she was a girl who found real people much more exciting than the characters in any story.

He worked with concentration for some minutes and

then was startled into a blot by his master's voice behind him. "Ah, good, good, I want those finished."

Hylas got on with his work, but the senator continued to fuss around the room. He had the kind of presence one could never ignore. Large, red-faced, and awkward in his movements, he was often irritable with slaves and children, but he was not a fool. He saw things too clearly black or white to have much political judgment, but he could appreciate faithfulness and intelligence and, except during his rages, treated Hylas well enough.

The senator had ended up in front of the cupboard at the far end of the room. Some of the scrolls were stored in especially made boxes and some in leather cases. He opened two, looked at the title tags, and then turned back to Hylas. "Have you checked these recently?"

"Yes, my lord, I had everything out and the cupboard was cleaned and tidied at the end of last month."

"Last month? Nothing was missing or in the wrong place?"

"No, my lord. The Gallic Wars of the Divine Caesar were torn and I sent the scroll to be repaired—had you been looking for it?"

"No, not that, never mind. I just wondered if anything had slipped in unnoticed—papers or tablets I had been working on."

He moved a couple of cases and put them back in a restless way and then strode over to the door. "If you found anything, you would—yes, of course you would. I've never known you careless." He turned in the door with as near a look of approval as Hylas had ever had from him.

"Thank you, my lord," he said, but the man had already gone.

Hylas put his pen down and sat rubbing his cramped fingers and wondering what was bothering his master. He thought back to how the room had looked when he had come in. Yes, his papers had been moved to one side as if Caius Pomponius had been there while he was away and had spread out a scroll or a map on the table. Perhaps something had got mixed up with his work. He looked through the pile of documents he was working from and under the tablets with his rough calculations. Nothing; whatever it was was not in the library. He moved the lamp nearer and bent over the last columns of figures.

The main courses of the family dinner had been served when he went down the steps to the kitchen an hour later. It was warm there after the chill of the April night above. The big oven was still glowing, and so was the charcoal grill on which a sucking pig had been roasted. Most of the slaves were up in the courtyard hoping for pickings from the serving table in the colonnade outside the dining room, but the cook was asleep in a corner now that his work was done. Nissa, Hylas's mother, was quietly collecting the things for Domina Faustina's night tray.

She brought him broken bread and half a chicken that was hardly touched, and then sat down to watch him eat. Times like this were the nearest to a home life that he had ever known, born as a slave in the house and cared for by Nissa in the odd moments she could snatch from attending her mistress.

Hylas was hungry, but when he had the chicken leg nearly clean he looked up at her, tall and gentle, with her once dark hair now nearly gray.

"Why's the master so jumpy, and why is Decianus staying to dinner here all of a sudden?"

"Hush, why shouldn't he be here? He's the mistress's son, after all."

"Maybe, but that doesn't mean he and the master like each other. Mother, I was thinking earlier, this house is getting like a sleeping volcano. You know, it's all very quiet, with the trees growing and the cattle grazing, and then there's a little rumble. People look up, but it stops and they forget it. It comes again, louder, but they're getting used to it and they hardly notice. Then, one day—woof— the top of the mountain blows off."

"I thought things were quieter since Blandina left."

"For you they are. It must be quite dull with just the mistress."

Nissa smiled, as if after fifteen years of Blandina dullness was more than welcome. Then there was a clatter as two of the houseboys who had been waiting at table came down the stairs giggling at each other.

"Just listen to that," said the one with the grin and the gap between his front teeth.

"How can we, with you making so much noise?" snapped Hylas.

Then they could all hear the raised voices, and the sudden clatter of a small table knocked over.

"Surely they're not fighting," said Nissa. "No, Hylas, wait." For he already had one foot on the steps to go and see what was happening, before he remembered the earliest lesson she had taught him: slaves keep out of trouble.

"Which of them started it, was it the master or Decianus?" he asked the boys, but they were giggling again. The news, whatever it was, would come first to the kitchen anyway; it was warm and private. Sure enough, there were more steps on the stairs—Aulus, the master's valet, a small man with a gray, unhealthy tinge to his skin. Hylas liked him; they served the same man and had been able to help each other from time to time.

"Whatever's upset Caius Pomponius?" he asked, smiling. Then he saw that Aulus's face was wet with sweat and his mouth was trembling. The man was really frightened.

"Castor and Pollux, I don't know. I don't honestly. It happened so fast. They were talking quietly enough, the two of them and Madam, and I'd just turned away to pick up the wine jug, when the master was on his feet shouting. Then the boys skipped off and Madam stood up with a face like Medusa and it was she who knocked the table over as she went out. Then Assinius pushed me out after her and shut the door in my face. And it's the Ides tomorrow, we shall have a happy holiday!"

"I must go to my mistress," said Nissa, picking up her tray and slipping off up the steps.

"But what were they talking about? You must have heard something," said Hylas.

"Not much, I don't listen when it's politics. That's got no interest for the likes of me—only when it's gossip from the Circus. Honestly, Hylas, I don't know, except that Decianus said something like, 'You can't have, Caius, not even you, we must have been crazy.' He said it quiet, though—that was probably why I noticed."

"Look, sit down and have a drink. I'll go and see what's happening now, or they'll be bellowing for someone and we won't hear. The house seems to be in enough trouble without one of us getting beaten."

It was quiet above, in the peristyle, and suddenly dark after the warm glow of the kitchen below. Some instinct warned him not to go through to the atrium, where he would be seen by anyone leaving the house, but to wait in the deeper shadow where a vine looped low between two pillars of the peristyle colonnade. There were lamps hanging outside the dining room and he could see the shut door, but almost before his eyes had adjusted to the faint light the double doors were flung back and two shapes had passed out of sight in the direction of the main door.

Hylas heard the startled clatter as the waiting slaves got up hurriedly from where they had been squatting by their litter outside the porter's room, playing knucklebones. There were voices, Decianus's nasal tones and a sharp word from Assinius the steward, and then the outer door shut and the iron bolts clanged into place. Hylas waited a moment longer, but Assinius did not come back, so he walked quietly as far as the dining-room door and looked in, standing well back.

Someone had picked up the table, but the furniture looked wrong, with the two couches out of line and the cushions thrown back where the diners had got up quickly. But Caius Pomponius was sitting down again, and for a moment Hylas thought that his master had seen him, he was gazing so fixedly at the doorway. Then he understood that what his master could see inside his head was something so vivid and terrifying that it had blotted out everything else. Hylas tiptoed past into the atrium, to the stairs that led to the attic where he slept with the other men. He had recognized the look in his master's eyes now, he had seen it already that day. It had been on the face of the slave on the building site as he gazed at the body across the pile of bricks and waited for the overseer.

III

AULUS

HYLAS WOKE, as he usually did, before dawn, when the man who rented the shop built into the house to the right of the front gate took down his shutters. It was a cookshop, and he did noisy business with the drivers who had brought carts to the great market during the night. It was still dark in the small attic where Hylas slept, and he lay half asleep for a time, till the memory of the disastrous end to last night's dinner came to him. Then he had the sinking feeling that comes when one has woken up cheerful and then remembered unpleasant things.

The first sounds of a household waking up came from below. The main door squeaked open as the porter let out the slave who went to the early market. Water splashed across the pavement of the atrium and there was the scratching of a broom. That was the young houseboy who hummed through his irregular teeth. From the back of the house came a clattering of pots, and the morning smells of smoke and fresh bread. It was cold in the attic beneath the tiles, but the kitchen would be better. Hylas threw off his blanket, straightened his tunic, and groped for the sandals that had been kicked under the bed. As he stood fastening his belt, a cry came from somewhere, no louder than the racket that already sounded from the street outside except that its tone, sharp and piercing, had cut through the noise like a yell of pain through party laughter.

The cry came only once, but after it came the silence, all the small noises of the house cut off, as if a door had been closed. Hylas found that, without thinking, he was at the top of the narrow stairs that led down to the corner of the atrium. There was some light there, shining from the lamps that had been lit for the morning's housework. He took the stairs three at a time; below, on the far side of the atrium, the houseboy was standing, staring back toward the pillared entry that led to the peristyle. Beyond, where the first glow of dawn shone down into the farther courtyard, there was a frieze of figures, the cook and his boy, two of the women. Between them under the cornice that topped the columns of red-marble, clear in the light of a lamp, stood Aulus, with one hand outstretched before him as if to receive a gift. He was staring down at it, and the eyes of every slave in both courtyards followed his, for the hand was as red and dark as the marble.

Hylas started toward him, and the movement seemed to release the bond of fear that had held the other slaves still. Aulus stumbled forward and fell on his knees beside the fish tank in the center of the atrium, plunging his whole arm into the water between the lily leaves. At the same time he began to cry, the wheezing sob of a small child who will howl louder when he has got his breath.

Hylas shook him as one shakes a small child to stop the noise. "Who is it?"

There was death in Aulus's face, and more deaths than one, but he did not answer. The women behind were whimpering now. Where was the steward? He ought to have been there to take charge. Hylas ran through into the peristyle.

The bedroom belonging to the master of the house was next door to the library. The light was growing fast now in a clear sky, and the glow from the lamp that Aulus had lit when he was laying out his master's toilet things before waking him seemed thin and yellow. The carved bed was under the window, its cover woven with purple and red, and the floor was inlaid with an intricate mosaic pattern of plaited bands; otherwise Aulus must have seen at once the small dark pool that lay just at the edge of the shadow under the bed.

The senator lay on his side, facing the door, but with his head buried in his arms. A corner of the cover trailed toward the floor, but the rest had become tightly twisted around his body during the night while he slept. Now the power of the master's physical presence was stronger than the memory of Aulus's hand and the small ambiguous stain on the floor. Hylas stood still, sick and shivering on the doorstep, till the sound of a shriek from the women's gallery sent him across the room to bend over the couch, one respectful hand plucking at his master's bare right arm. The flesh was cold and flaccid under his fingers. Poised on the left arm that had been beneath him, Caius Pomponius slid over on his back.

He had lain in a puddle of blood that must have been soaking slowly through the mattress for hours. His under-tunic was hideous with it, but the blank face with half-closed eyes was unmarked. Out of the dark, sodden folds plastered to his stomach and the fat above his ribs stuck something small and angled, forced deep into the flesh by the weight of the body that had rolled over on top of it. Hylas's hand went out, but he did not touch what he saw. Instead he glanced back at the toilet things arranged on the chest. It was a small knife, one of the set Aulus would have used with the comb and shears that still lay there, to trim his master's nails and hair before he went out to do the day's business. It was no wonder that there had been more than one death in Aulus's eyes as he had confronted his fellow slaves in the atrium, for that small ivory handle would destroy him as surely as it had done his master.

And only him? Hylas drew back into the shadows where the thick door curtains were looped back, as Domina Faustina's voice sounded outside. As she entered the room, swathed to the ankles in the dark-blue cloak she had thrown on over her tunic, she looked like a queen of the underworld, but Hylas did not stop to watch her shock and grief. He had edged around the doorpost past two half-dressed women and into the familiar sanctuary of his library next door.

The curtain fell back behind him, and he was alone with his desk and the shelves of scrolls and the busts of former senators in their tall alcoves. The noise outside was appalling now; every woman in the house seemed to be shrieking her head off. Suddenly Domina Faustina's voice sounded, clear and dominating.

"Is there no man left alive here?"

Someone answered, the voice high-pitched and disjointed with terror. What now? Hylas knew what would happen, and he realized that his ears were already straining for the sounds that must surely come soon.

Above the normal hubbub of the street that had risen to a roar as an excited crowd heard the words of death shrieked from an upper window came the thudding of heavy boots marching, not breaking step in the narrow alleys as the way opened before them, the guard from the market.

As they ground to a halt outside the main gate, the women's wailing hushed to a whimper. The shock and terror seemed to have made a stillness inside Hylas's head as well, so that the noises outside came from a long way off. In that unnatural silence he heard a voice; it was Caius himself speaking to a friend not a month before as they discussed the recent murder of the city prefect by a slave. "But the principle must be upheld. If you have a poisoned wound, do you leave it to infect the whole body? No, you cauterize it, so that the evil humors may be destroyed once and for all. A slave who has killed is like poison in the veins of a household; when he dies his companions must die with him. Four or four hundred, it is the law, or the household could infect the whole city. There can be no exceptions to the general sentence of death."

Caius was dead, and Aulus, though still living, would when the knife was found in the body be as utterly destroyed as his master. If there was time for him to use another on himself before his arms were pinioned by the guard, then his length of pain would be briefer but its end no less certain. Yet Hylas, too, had seen the knife and others had watched while he had entered the room. There were loud voices outside in the peristyle; by the sound of it the guards were herding the slaves across from the master's room into the dining room. There was only one door, and no window into the alley beyond; one man with a sword could guard it.

"Proclus! Up there, go through the women's rooms." The harsh voice was the thickness of a curtain away.

Hylas gave one quick look at the window above him, but the bars across it were set in concrete and already the regular step of a sentry passed below it on the other side of the wall. There was only one place in the room large enough to conceal a man, a niche high on the wall to the left of the door.

The most impressive of the portrait busts of the early Pomponii were, according to custom, kept in alcoves off the atrium. Here, banished to a lesser place, was the bust of a cousin two generations back who had disgraced the family. Old Quintus had not only removed the bust from the public rooms but ordered a tapestry curtain to be hung on a rod across the niche where it stood.

Hylas got his foot up on the lower shelf of the scroll cabinet and hung there while he stuck his head behind the curtain. There was certainly not enough room by normal standards for a man, but he was thin and frightened enough to attempt impossible feats.

The dusty top of the cabinet was above eye level; a quick inspection by the guard would not show that anyone had stood there. Half kneeling, he coiled himself around the bust like a statue of Apollo and one of the unwilling nymphs of mythology. The curtain swung back flat against the wall. There was no sign of niche or slave when the guard entered the library just long enough afterward for Hylas's panting breaths to have grown quieter.

It depended now on whether the guard first looked left or right, for Domina Faustina, with a love of symmetry, had hung an identical curtain at the other end of the room, and that covered a blank wall. If he took the trouble to look behind that one first, he would be unlikely to look behind the other.

There was a metallic scraping noise from the other end of the room. Straining to hear above the noisy pounding of his own heart, Hylas could almost see the lance stuck up negligently to move the curtain back. The sound stopped, the footsteps moved back toward the door.

Hylas dug his face into his left shoulder to stifle the small snicker he could not control. With the great clarity of helplessness and terror, he had seen a quick vision of Claudius, the former Emperor, as he had been described so many times on the day of the assassination of the Emperor Gaius. He had been caught by the guard behind a curtain in the palace because his feet were sticking out, and hauled off to be proclaimed Emperor himself. Hylas's feet had not stuck out, and his fate if the guard caught up with him would be far more distressing.

The room was empty now, although confused noises continued to come from the peristyle outside. Hylas eased his position slightly. It made the curtain bulge, but it was either that or fall out of the niche completely. Now, if ever in his life quick thinking had saved him, it must do it again.

Caius was dead. That fact could be set aside to be considered later; someone had killed him, but Domina Faustina had summed up that problem when she had said, "Is there no man left alive here?" There were no men now in the Villa Pomponia except the slaves. The master was dead, his son was in Germany. So Caius had been killed either by a slave or by someone from outside the house, and Hylas knew which alternative the overworked praetor was likely to favor.

Then death lay on the ten men and six women of the household as certainly as if they had been shut in with a plague victim. To judge by the wailing outside, they were already being marched away. He could hear the noise the housekeeper was making, a fat, rather silly woman who always cried when things went wrong. It was only then that he remembered Nissa. She would not make a sound, she was probably trying to comfort the housekeeper now even while she was being driven to prison and death, and he could not reach her with the comfort she should have had from her son. She was going out through the gates of the villa while he hid behind a curtain and wept because he was helpless. And at any moment someone might cry out, "Where's Hylas?" and he, too, would be lost with her. Madam would certainly be asked for a list of the household and then, at the latest, he would be missed.

Was there any chance that when the house was searched again he might no longer be there? Inside Hylas's usually mild and well-ordered heart, as he crouched in the dusty niche, something small and hard and unexpected had already started to form. If he was caught he would die, but if he was not caught and there was any power in Rome that could help him, the other slaves should not die either. He was certain that no man from among them would have killed the master and no woman would have had the strength; the injustice of their deaths was intolerable. Such determination seemed ridiculous, but it was enough to stop him running out after them in despair.

It was quiet outside now. Only the guards paced ceaselessly around the peristyle and outside the window, their tread muffled by the street noises that had come with full daylight. By the end of the second hour the news would be all over Rome, passed through the packed terraces of the Circus as the second day of the games started. It would reach Camillus and Blandina, and then Decianus and the rest of the family, and then the senators who were allied in friendship or common interest with the family of the Pomponii. Soon the house would be full again, for the centurion of the guard would not move the body without the authority of some member of the family.

Perhaps then there would be an opportunity. There were three ways out of the house. The front and side doors were guarded: the third way—over the roofs—was probably impossible, but as the least impossible of the three it needed consideration. Hylas began to give it that.

IV

VARRO

THE LAST OF the senators did not leave the villa until after noon. By then it was a beautiful spring day with a cloudless sky and warm sun. The shadows cast by the pillars around the peristyle lay across the colonnade as dark and sharp as they did in summer, and the air in the small bedroom, where the blood had dried on the mattress in dark cakes and flies crawled, was heavy and stinking with the excitement of those who had come to peer and shudder.

Hylas was watching the open courtyard from above. The sun was beating down on the back of his head and his bare legs as he lay pressed flat into the gulley behind the low parapet that supported a row of ornamental urns edging the roof above the women's gallery. He had reached this safe but uncomfortable place by using the rule most slaves learn early—no one usually questions a slave who seems busy already. He had only had to cross the width of the peristyle to the partly curtained archway that led to the bottom of the women's stairs. The slaves and hangers-on had moved aside for Hylas as he came out of the library carrying a large box full of scrolls, the tagged handles of which stuck up high enough partly to conceal his face. Once he was around the turn of the stairs, the most difficult part was over.

The guards had already searched the women's rooms and he had the whole upper floor to himself. From the confusion in Domina Faustina's room, someone had already been to collect what she would need while she stayed —where? Probably with her son Decianus and daughter-in-law Livonia. Hylas knew that at any moment someone might come up the stairs, but half an hour now could make a great difference to his chance of staying free after he escaped. He went through the women's rooms carefully, wriggling from one to the other on his stomach below the level of the balustrade. In this way he was able not only to finish his mistress's breakfast but to find a little food and water to take with him to his present safe but uncomfortable hiding place on the roof, reached from a trap door in the attic. From the attic he had collected a few small belongings in the leather satchel he used to carry writing things outside the house. His own savings were locked in the steward's brass-bound coffer and he regretted them very much.

It was hard to tell if he could be seen from the balconies of the insula on the other side of the courtyard, but he thought the parapet was too high. Several women had spent the last hour hanging over to stare at the activity below them, and they would certainly have shouted and pointed if they had seen him. Now there were far too many hours ahead in which to wonder how he would be received when he tried to climb out that way after darkness fell. And that was the only way he could go, with the guards patrolling the outer walls of the house. The clear-headedness of the morning had gone and his mind felt feverish and confused. He was sick with fear and with worry for his mother and with the sheer discomfort of his position. Hylas dropped his head on his arms and tried to sleep.

It took the best part of an hour, after dusk fell, to work his way around below the level of the parapet to the wall of the insula. The fourth floor directly above him was smooth, but at each corner on the fifth was a balcony. A lamp shone behind the shutters of the one on his left, but the other was still dark and festooned with pots of plants. Something about the sight of the growing things made him study this one more hopefully. Whoever watered them all so carefully was perhaps a person more likely to receive him kindly than the strangers behind the lighted shutters, and the dark room might even be empty. Now the problem was to climb in without knocking a rose bush down on the head of the guard who still stood watch below.

Hylas tied the satchel firmly against his back with a spare belt and began to look for toe holds in the flaking plaster between the wooden beams of the wall. It was a climb that he could not have made in daylight, but now, with the surface just in front of his eyes, not looking beyond the next reach of his hand, he thought he could do it. Halfway, a beam stuck out a palm's breadth, and he hung on to it for some minutes without the strength to get his knee up on it and reach for the rafters that supported the balcony.

Then, when he lay against the wall, his foot safe on the beam, drying sweat-slippery hands on the seat of his tunic for the last heave up, a little dust fell on his upturned face and there was the scraping of a pot being moved just above his head.

"Got to mind the old lady's rose tree!" said a man's voice softly, hardly above a breath. "Still now, the centurion's just come out."

Hylas froze flat as a lizard against the wall, where the balcony cast a deeper shadow from the faint glow of the city that lit the sky even on cloudy nights.

"Quick now, give us your hand."

Hylas reached up blindly in the darkness. Strong fingers closed around his wrist and another hand caught the neck of his tunic, pulling it almost over his head. He came across the edge of the balcony so fast that he scraped the skin off his knees and landed in a heap on the floor.

The man who now stood above him began to sing loudly, with the nasal, keening note of a drunk after the last-but-one cup. His voice tailed off halfway through the second verse of "The Girls of Ostia." The rose was back in its place by now.

"In you go," he said, pushing the shutter back.

The room behind the balcony was in darkness except for the faint light that came through an open doorway at the back, leading to the communal staircase.

"Don't move now," said the voice again. "The old lady doesn't like her pots knocked over." And Hylas, who had been aware of the looming of unseen shapes in the darkness, froze still, as a lamp was lit from the pink glow in the ashes of a charcoal stove. The shadows streamed away from the tiny light between blackened rafters festooned as thickly as a grape arbor in October with hanging bundles and bunches. Except for the plastered shelf that must be the bed and a couple of stools, there was no other furniture, but as Hylas had guessed, the room was crowded with baskets and jars and—almost as solid as the baskets—a texture of smells that caught in his throat and made him cough. There was the human smell of bedding and smoldering charcoal and bread, but interlacing above it was every herb he had ever been dosed with or had smelled in the house-keeper's linen chests.

There were heavy, slow footsteps outside on the landing, and as the lamp burned brighter, the large outline of an old woman came into the room, fussing a little as she pulled the door shut behind her and dropped the beam. Hylas faced the two strangers together.

"So you got him, Varro?" said an old but forceful voice. "Now, let's have a look, which was he?"

Hylas looked at the man first. Older than he was, though not by many years, and not tall, but wiry, with a pointed face and two broken teeth. He grinned at Hylas.

"The old lady's been watching you most of the day. She knows everyone in the household as if they were neighbors, now she can't get down the stairs at all. What's your name? You're the secretary one, aren't you? At first I thought you were the tall thin lad who does the lamps."

"Yes, I'm the secretary. They call me Hylas."

"That's Matidia, she's my aunt. I work in the market and sleep here most days, it's nearer than my mother's place."

The old woman began to potter around in a comforting way with water to wash his dusty hands and head and a thin wine to cool his dry throat. He moved over to the bed and curled his feet up so that he could lean back against the wall. Slowly his tense body relaxed. He was almost asleep. Varro had drawn him in out of the darkness to safety and a welcome. It was more than enough for the moment, far more than he had ever dreamed of during the hot hours on the roof. What power had directed him to this one room and why he had been received he was beyond considering sensibly. When Varro spoke, the voice seemed to come from a long way away.

"So who did it, then?"

"Killed the master? What are they saying?"

"That one of you did it. But he wasn't that bad, was he?"

"No. By Zeus no, not bad enough for that. Not bad enough for a knife deep in by someone who hated him."

"It was a knife, then? You saw him? They say he was badly hacked about."

"No, I didn't see anything like that, though there wasn't time to look properly. It looked to me like once in the right place."

Varro tilted his stool back and considered this. "Then it would have to be someone who knew. I've seen fights in the market. It can take nothing at all to kill a man, one jab aimed right or the corner of a stall catching the back of his head. And then another time two Nubians went at each other with meat choppers. Like the arena it was—blood everywhere, but it didn't kill either of them; they weren't thinking where they put the blows. Well then, who did do it?"

"I don't know. Every time I try to think about it my mind seems to knot up and I can't think properly."

"That's not going to help those poor women in prison tonight, and one of them's your mother, isn't she? We thought that was why you were escaping."

"Yes, but how can I do anything?" Hylas asked, twisting his hands between his knees. "If I'm caught in the streets, I'll be killed with the rest of them."

Varro looked at him hard, and he had steady eyes. "Listen, Hylas, I think you're the kind of lad I took you for when I first saw you hiding down there. I can see you've been too scared so far to have thought straight, but you've had a good education and that ought to help now, or why have you had the good luck to be saved? I know you didn't do it, anyone who bothers to look at you can see that, but a man was killed down there last night in his own house, and that's a bad thing. What's worse is that in this city, with him being a slaveowner, unless a thunderbolt splits the roof of the prison, a lot of people who never did any harm except to lose their freedom are going to die too."

"I know that!"

"All right, you know it. I could get you out of here in the morning and clear of the city by whatever road you chose. Or we can try to think if there is any way you can help those poor souls in prison. Now, you really don't know who did it? It can't have been an accident."

"I don't see who it could have been, that's the trouble. There was only Domina Faustina in the house except for the master and the rest of us. That is when Decianus Gallus had left after the quarrel."

"Yes, what was that about, dear? I could hear something even from up here," said the old woman.

"I don't know, I wasn't in the dining room, but the master and his brother shouted at each other and the mistress was very displeased. But Decianus left immediately afterward, I saw him go, so there was nobody strange left in the villa, and I heard the porter lock the door."

"Well, it seems peculiar," said Varro. "A family row and then the senator's found dead in the morning!"

Hylas looked up slowly at the face opposite him. "Oh, Zeus, I think he saw it, I think the master saw his own death last night. I watched him sitting there and I understood some of what he was feeling, but not this, not this death."

"Wasn't there anyone else in the dining room, any of the other slaves?" asked Varro.

"Only Assinius, he pushed the others out. That's strange, I didn't see him at all this morning, after Aulus found the body. I wonder where he was. Still, he must have been taken away with the rest of them."

"I didn't see him," said the old woman.

"But he must have been there, and he could tell us what this is about. He's the only person to know, and it's no good trying to prove a slave didn't do it without knowing who did. We would never be believed."

Hylas's hands were tightly clasped on his knees, and now he put his head down almost to touch them, so that those penetrating eyes on the other side of the glow from the small lamp would not see that his mouth was trembling. There was no help really, it was a waste of time even to talk about it; and he had a good imagination, too good at the moment. He did not need to be told what was probably happening even now at the prison; would they have questioned the women yet?

As if he could read Hylas's mind, Varro said, "What we need is someone who could go to the prison and find out who is there, and if Assinius is with them. If there was someone who cared enough about the family to take the trouble."

Hylas thought about that, not sensibly, going over possible names, but almost in a dream; and from somewhere deep in his mind he found that he was looking at someone.

He sat bolt upright, his eyes suddenly blazing. Some god had blessed him with an inspiration for the second time in one day.

"Camillus Rufus!"

"The young tribune who married little Madam? But he wouldn't take any notice of us, would he? And wouldn't he hand you over to the guard if he knew you were free?"

"He owes me something. I know it sounds silly, but he does. It was only yesterday that he told me to ask if I ever needed a favor. He might refuse to help, but he wouldn't give me up, not without a try."

"Where would I find him in the morning? What barber does he use?"

"Figulus, at the bottom of the Sandalmakers' Street. The sign of the silver shears."

"You could write something for me to give to him. Do it now, so I can take it early. We haven't much time. Hours count when four large guards are kicking you. You brought your pens, didn't you?"

Yes, thought Hylas, I brought my pens, what secretary wouldn't? Writing letters is all I'm good for. Even this man who's only seen my mother from five floors up can do more for her than I can. The small, hard, determined thing that had first started to form that morning in the library was getting large. He had been shamed by Varro, and now there was nothing else that could be done, except to write this letter, for the rest of the night, while he would lie safe and be able to think in one dark room what was being done in that other darkness.

"Why?" he asked Varro, looking up at the man, feeling sick and shaken and very small. "What is all this about? I'm putting you both in danger and you're not a rich man, you can't afford the risk of sheltering an escaped slave."

"Why not? Perhaps I'm the sort of man who saves unwanted puppies from drowning and then gets left with them. There's another reason, but perhaps I'll tell you that later."

The old woman bustled out of the shadows from among the bundles on the other side of the room, where she had been busying herself. A cup steamed pungently in her hands. "Now, son, you need sleep or you won't be fit to help anyone in the morning. You drink this down, and if you don't sleep, I'm losing my skill, and after seventy-two years."

V

CAMILLUS

CAMILLUS TILTED his head over so that the barber could get at his right cheek and kept very still indeed; Figulus was carrying on an excited conversation over the top of his head as he shaved him, and he was not too steady with a razor at the best of times. Camillus wondered, as he did nearly every day, why he came to this barber out of the many who were in Rome, but it was near his house and his friends came, and almost all barbers were equally awful. Perhaps by the time he was praetor he would be able to afford his own.

People were talking about only one thing this morning; even the crash in the fifth chariot race yesterday had received only a passing mention. Camillus had said little, except to give accurate information about how his father-in-law had died. He could tell that the rest of the crowd of regulars would be glad when he went, so they could talk more freely than was possible before a member of the family.

He noticed that Galerius was speaking to a workman who had eased himself past the crowd at the counter, who were trying out the latest Persian rose essence, to the bench at the back of the shop where customers waited for Figulus. Camillus saw that they were both looking his way. The man made a polite gesture that was almost a bow, and Galerius was left with a small scroll in his hands.

When Figulus had finished with him, Camillus paid with as good a grace as he could muster after the scraping his chin had received, and went across to his friend. Galerius passed over the scroll.

"For you. Strange, the man wouldn't wait."

Camillus sat down and unrolled it. The writing was excellent, and that in itself was unusual considering the appearance of the man who had delivered it. Also it was in Greek, which suggested that it was private. He read it carefully twice, stroking his tingling face with a finger as he did so.

"To the noble tribune Camillus Rufus, greetings. May Zeus himself, dispenser of justice, grant you prosperity and further my just cause with you. The innocent household of Caius Pomponius Afer implores the help of the friend of their new master, Marcus Pomponius. The bearer of this letter will bring you to a place where I can tell you more fully what I know about the death of my master. In token of my trust this letter places my life in your hands. Farewell. Hylas, secretary in the household of Caius Pomponius Afer."

Camillus let the scroll curl up and pushed it into the deep fold of his toga.

"Business?" asked Galerius.

"I don't know. I suppose you could call it that. Not pleasure, anyway," Camillus said thoughtfully. "Something I must look into. I couldn't have come to the Circus today anyhow, I'm supposed to be in mourning."

They parted outside the shop. Camillus stood in the doorway and looked both ways up the street. As he had expected, after a few moments the man could be seen behind the festoons of sandals hanging around the booth of a shoemaker farther up the hill. *Sizing me up to see if I* look like calling the guard, thought Camillus. The man stared hard at him and then turned away and began to elbow his way, not too fast, through the crowds that were going down toward the Circus.

Camillus followed. It was not difficult to keep the man in sight, because he paused at each corner before turning into the maze of alleys below the Caelian Hill. Poor young Hylas, he had not remembered him when he had first heard of the arrest of the slaves the morning before, but that was not surprising, as he had been dealing with a hysterical young wife for the next few hours. Still, he had spoken to Hylas two days ago, and he owed the boy a hearing now. It was little enough to repay the quick thinking that had saved him from injury. Remembering the accident, Camillus lost his man in the crowd.

Then he saw that a patrol of Praetorians was coming. It would have been easy to stop them, and that was clearly why his guide was no longer in sight. Camillus paused to look at the lamp stands outside a bronzesmith's shop, and when he glanced up again, the man had decided that all was clear and was lounging at the corner at the top of the alley.

He knew they must be near the house of Caius Pomponius, but the maze of narrow passages in which he found himself was unfamiliar. He had almost caught up with his guide by the time the man turned in under the archway that led to the main stairs of a large block of cheap rooms. Camillus had seldom been in such a place, and the stinks and darkness, the hum and clatter of people squashed too close together oppressed him. It was a tall block and they had climbed to the fourth floor before the man stopped and faced him for the first time. Clearly he would not even now show the tribune where Hylas waited for him without making sure of his intentions.

"He said he could trust you, but he's only a lad and I have to think of myself and the old lady," he said.

It did not make full sense, but Camillus guessed what he meant. "This much I promise you, I will never bring the guard here. What more can I say until I understand what has happened?"

The man seemed satisfied. He led the way up one more flight of stairs and then knocked quietly on a door. Feet shuffled behind it and the bolt was drawn back. Camillus found himself inside the room ahead of his guide and the door bolted behind him. He had a quick prickle of danger up his spine and then something more powerful than fear took over, a keen interest in what was about to happen.

It was a dark and cluttered room that he saw; the old woman who had opened the door sat herself down again on a stool pulled near the light that came in from a balcony, and picked up the bowl of herbs she had been shredding. Hylas had got up quickly from the bed and Camillus saw the slim, neat young Greek with dark hair standing very tense with his hands clenched at his sides. Clearly he had been shaken now out of a lifetime of unobtrusiveness and was uncertain how to behave. What he did do surprised Camillus very much.

With a movement that could only have been made by a Greek he dropped to one knee, took Camillus's hand, and laid it against his forehead. It was a gesture old as supplication itself. Camillus bent over and took him by the shoulders to raise him. Now that they were face to face, Hylas was still dumb with distress. Camillus looked around him;

old Matidia said nothing to help and Varro was leaning back against the door with his hands folded.

"How did you get here?" Camillus asked. Best to start with something simple. "The gates were guarded."

For the first time Hylas's face almost relaxed. "I'll show you, but be careful, please."

He led Camillus to the balcony; even standing well back, partly hidden behind the pots of roses and herbs in hanging baskets, they could see down into the peristyle of the house below. A guard, leaning against one of the red-marble pillars, was picking his teeth, but otherwise the house seemed deserted.

"Still so close?" asked Camillus. And yet when he came to think of it, it was a clever hiding place, for even if the slave was already being searched for, this was an unlikely place for him still to be in. He would have expected Hylas to be far away by now and more likely to be picked up by a road patrol beyond the city gates than to be still in sight of the place where his master was murdered.

"How could I leave the city yet, before they . . . before the end of the games? My mother was taken with the other slaves, my lord," said Hylas, answering his unspoken thought.

"But where were you when the body was found? Surely you didn't get out of the house before then?"

Hylas told him. Varro had brought up the other stool for the tribune and then gone back to his post by the door, but the slave stood tense with embarrassment, like a recruit before his officer, as he went hour by hour through the story of the previous day.

It took some time, because Camillus wanted to be quite sure of the details, but before they were halfway through he found himself considering the slave with a new respect. He had guessed that the lad was intelligent; strange how he automatically thought of Hylas as much younger than himself, although there could not have been more than a year between their ages. Pomponius had been lucky to produce such a secretary from within his own household, and one who had already shown a strength of character and common sense that was not often found among the slave-born, who had never had to think for themselves. He had not only avoided arrest but had already managed to collect his shattered wits enough to consider more than his own danger. When at last Hylas seemed to have finished, Camillus sat for a moment longer arranging his own thoughts and wondering if he himself would have done half so well.

Hylas stood looking down at him, trying to see into his mind. His stomach seemed to jump painfully when Camillus grinned suddenly and said, "For pity's sake sit down. I'm getting a stiff neck looking up at you!"

Hylas sat down on the bed with a bump and then clasped his hands to stop them trembling. "Have you been with the members of the family since yesterday morning, my lord?" he asked. "Was anything said about me?"

"No, I've been occupied most of the time with my wife, but we heard nothing of any member of the household being missing. Of course, someone should have counted the slaves at once and checked that you were all there, but without Assinius, whose word the guard would have trusted, I suppose that was difficult. But before we try to understand that, let's look at the main problem; everyone is assuming that a slave killed your master because they were the only people in the house except for his mother. You say it wasn't a slave; if not, who was it? Someone coming in from outside? Then we've got to guess who it was and be able to prove it, or it will be much more convenient just to hush things up and execute the slaves."

"How long before it happens?" asked Hylas in a small, flat voice.

Camillus counted on his fingers. "Yesterday was the Ides. The games started the day before and last eight days. There can be no court hearing before the twentieth, when there is one clear day before the Festival of Rome. Even if there is no proper murder trial, there must be an inquiry, and that can't be held till the courts open for business. Your fellow slaves are safe from death till then."

"From death, yes."

Camillus saw that Hylas was remembering how evidence was obtained and the ways the guards used to make sure it agreed. Yes, death would come to mean something rather different to someone who had already spent some days in the hands of the imperial inquiry agents.

The room went quiet, so that Camillus could hear a woman shouting at her child through the thin wall to the next flat. Then he looked at Hylas, who was staring out at the balcony. As a boy he had always been one for sudden enthusiasms and difficult causes, and now it seemed that pattern was being repeated again. Here he was, newly married and due in ten days to start north to rejoin his legion; it was bad enough that he must spend part of the time officially in mourning for a man he had not known well or liked particularly. But when he arrived in camp, there would be Marcus to be faced and what was he to tell him? "Yes, your father was killed by a slave, so the whole household has been executed, what a shame. I did have the chance to look into things but it was too much trouble. Never mind, when you come home to be married yourself, you can reopen the house again and everything will be all right." Besides, it was his wife's father who had been killed, and she was still sobbing her heart out over him. Camillus had been surprised that she had shown so much grief.

He realized that Hylas had grown embarrassed by his stare and had dropped his head, waiting to know what Camillus would do now. Yet was there any question, wasn't he already too deeply involved not to go further? He knew what he was going to have to do, because although a member of the Senate and the mother of a slave weighed against each other was hopeless odds, his school lessons on Roman justice still meant something to him. Also he owed Hylas a debt and he was something of a gambler; also there was the excitement and possible danger ahead. No, he was not making a prudent decision, but he didn't care.

"What did you hope to do next?" he asked. "You need to know a lot of things a slave couldn't find out even if he wasn't being chased by the guard. I suppose you were hoping I would ask the questions for you. Hylas, stop looking like that. You must have been fairly sure when you sent your message that I would help you."

Hylas wiped the back of his hand quickly across his face. "Last night I thought so, but this morning it seemed like a silly dream. Could you go to the prison, my lord, and find out how they are?"

"Yes, and who exactly is there and why they missed you yesterday in the house. We can't do anything else till we know that."

Camillus stood up and went over to the balcony to look down into the peristyle far below. "Two days ago we were sitting down there, and I was playing with my wife's monkey and Caius Pomponius was alive. And he seemed very much as usual, we were planning to go to the races together today. Hylas, you've asked yourself 'who' could have killed him. Have you wondered 'why'?"

"He quarreled with Decianus Gallus that evening."

"Did he now? I hadn't heard that."

Hylas smiled wearily. "That's hardly surprising, my lord. Would you spread the story around that you had had an argument with a murdered man a few hours before his death?"

"No, I suppose not."

"But my master was worried about something even before that dinner."

"How do you know? Did you hear him talk about it?"

"No," said Hylas. "That was partly what worried me. He wasn't a man to keep his thoughts to himself. It was what I first noticed, that he had become quieter. That last evening after you had gone he was looking for something, papers I think, and I'm sure he didn't find them."

"But how could anyone have got into that locked house in the night?" asked Camillus, starting to pace nervously backward and forward in the crowded room. "You found it hard enough to get out of. Could they have got in over the roofs?"

"No, dear," said Matidia unexpectedly, looking up from her herbs. "I would have seen them. I don't sleep much at nights now. A doze in the afternoon when I have to keep quiet because Varro is sleeping suits me much better. There was Madam, of course, wandering around down below like she often does. I don't think she sleeps any better than I do now."

Camillus had turned quickly on his heel at the sound of

her voice. Now he quieted his instinctive questions and pulled his stool over nearer her.

"What a shame to sleep so badly! You mean you sit out here all night sometimes, Granny?"

"Yes, I do, when it's warm enough. It was mild that night, and I saw the lady going to and fro around about midnight when they were all asleep, the porter and all."

"It's strange, your having seen her like that!" Camillus turned around and saw Hylas's face. The slave was staring straight in front of him as if he had been turned to stone. Then Camillus saw another still, stone-carved face in his own mind: Domina Faustina. He remembered something his wife had said once, giggling, "Oh, we all called her Medusa, my friends and I. I'm sure her stare used to curdle the milk." No, that was something not to be thought of yet, not until he had been to the prison and busied himself with practical things; and no, it was not something he could speak of yet, even to Hylas.

He stood up. "I must go, it's midmorning already. Don't expect to hear from me before evening. There may be other things I need to see to when I find out how the land lies."

Hylas shivered, came out of his dream, and stood up too. "And what can I do now? I can't stay here, it's not safe for Matidia and Varro."

"Who says that?" asked Varro, coming over from the door. "If they were going to search this block they would have done it by now, and even if they still do, there's any number of places I could hide you. You're as safe here as anywhere, at least till your beard grows."

Hylas put up his hand to the spiky two days' growth that was beginning to show strongly against his fair skin. It was going to be slow torment to sit here all day with Matidia, kind as she was.

"You must watch the house," said Camillus. "We don't know what we're looking for, so we can't afford to miss anything, even who comes and goes on the day of the funeral."

"It's today?"

"Yes, this evening, and high time too. Until then." He put out a hand and touched Hylas lightly on the shoulder as he had done before, and then walked quickly to the door. They heard his steps echoing down the wooden stairs.

Hylas and Varro looked at each other. "Well, you can pick your friends," said Varro.

VI

THE PRISON OF MACROBIUS

THE STENCH IN the insula where he had left Hylas had been bad, but that in the prison where Camillus finally found the household of Pomponius was something new in his experience. The prison had first been built as a warehouse and had only been converted because of its thick walls. But it had been an unlucky choice, for it was too near the river and the cellars had been dug in ground liable to flood, so that a miasma of damp mingled with and strengthened the other stenches.

However, Camillus began to feel lucky the moment he set eyes on the governor. He was a man whose face he knew well, a retired veteran centurion from his own legion. Macrobius had been hated by the men as a cruel flogger and a rigid disciplinarian, and that was a bad omen for the prisoners in his care, but the governor could have suspected none of this from the warmth of the tribune's greeting. This man's goodwill could be important to him.

"So you have the household of my unfortunate father-in-law here?" he said, after some warm reminiscences about garrison life.

"Yes, they were brought in yesterday morning. A miserable-looking lot they were, and I was hard put to it to fit them in. There was a riot last night outside the Circus— someone not settling his debts—and now I shall be full to the bursting point till the courts open again, even if we get through the rest of the festival without more trouble."

"A pious hope! Still, you can't expect slaves awaiting execution to be looking their best, Centurion. No doubt you received a checklist from the steward with no difficulty?"

"Well, that's just the trouble, sir, we were promised it but it didn't come. I know the family have their problems, with the son of the house away and the funeral of such an important man to arrange, but I have my responsibilities too and I ought to know who I'm supposed to be guarding."

The mention of the steward had raised no reaction. That was interesting. "I'll mention it again, Centurion," Camillus said, making a mental note to do nothing of the sort. "Now, perhaps, as a member of the family I could see the prisoners."

There seemed to be no difficulty about that. As Macrobius led the way down to the lower levels of the prison, Camillus was congratulating himself that so far his bluff of some official reason to be here had worked, and also that incredibly after a full day the governor still had no accurate list of the slaves. He had been right to feel lucky, because it seemed certain that Hylas had not yet been missed.

At the bottom of a flight of steps the stench, which had been noticeable even in the governor's room, reached its full strength. A large cellar had been divided with an iron grille into a number of cages, like the beast pits under the amphitheater. None was empty, but the prisoners in some were ragged humps who crouched far back from the pitch torches burning at irregular intervals. The guards even down here came smartly to attention, so it was clear that

Macrobius's discipline still extended to them and not only to the prisoners.

The household of Pomponius were together in the end cell, the one farthest from any gleam of light or fresh air.

"You keep the men and women together, I see."

"It's convenient with a batch like this. They won't be here long enough for it to make any problems. Now let's see, how many have we got, Quintus?"

"Fourteen, sir, eight men and six women. No, it's seven men now."

"Oh, yes, the valet, he died, didn't he? Pity, it was much too soon, I wasn't half finished with him. It's funny, sir, some of them will lie there shouting for death, while they've the strength to shout, and it won't come. Others—an hour, you've hardly touched them and they've gone. Witchcraft, I call it."

Camillus privately thought it was lucky that the miserable Aulus had proved to have a weak heart. Perhaps now that he was dead he could be made to carry the guilt, for a while at least; it would be no help in the end.

"Then that's it, isn't it, Macrobius," he said aloud. "Sometimes the gods do strike with justice; clearly his crime was more than he could bear. I suppose it's just a matter of confinement now for these poor wretches till after the hearing, and it will be six days till then."

"More or less. We need confirmation, of course, descriptions of how the man was seen coming from his master's room with his hands actually red with blood, red-handed you might say, but we're getting them."

Of course you are, thought Camillus. And, you oaf, how could anyone touch a man who'd been bleeding for hours, even at the rate blood comes from a corpse, and not get it all over him, particularly if the room was dark and he didn't know his master was a corpse anyway?

Macrobius took the key of the great lock that closed the door through the grille, and turned it. Most of the slaves pressed forward, straining in silence to hear what was being said, but from the back of the cell an unpleasant moaning continued, like the sobbing of a too much punished child.

"You'll not be long, sir?" asked Macrobius.

"Hardly. Centurion! Let's have that door opened quickly, please. I'm not talking to the prisoners through bars, and I don't want to spend the whole morning in this cesspit."

The slaves drew back as the door was swung open and then shut behind him. Camillus looked among the dirty, tear-stained faces and unshaved cheeks for someone he could talk to. Suddenly it came to him properly for the first time what he had taken on. This was not a schoolboy's test exercise in rhetoric, something to be put right just by talking. These people, the men and women in front of him, would die if he was slow-witted, and he would land himself in more trouble than he could easily handle, for there was more behind the death of his father-in-law than a simple mistake in the identity of the killer. Now he needed to find which of these bedraggled women was Hylas's mother. Not the old woman sobbing at the back or the girl clawing at his knees, anyway.

When he looked around again it was easy, even under the dirt. She was taller than he had expected, but they had the same eyes. He pointed to her. "You, come here."

Then they all crowded forward, but the woman seemed to have some inkling of what he wanted, and to have some authority left among her fellow slaves.

"No, better one at a time," she said. "Let go, you silly girl, that isn't helping anyone."

Then she straightened up and, to Camillus's great surprise, smiled at him. "We are glad to see you, noble Tribune, we had thought we were forgotten."

"You're Nissa," he said, and when she nodded her head, puzzled that he should know her name, he went on quietly. "The guards are watching us. Listen, but try not to show what you're thinking. You have a son, I believe?"

Her eyes widened and Camillus saw her hands jerk as if she would have raised them to her face but had stopped herself. Again she nodded.

"A son who is a secretary? I can name no names, they carry farther than words in a place like this. You understand me. You should be proud of your son, for it was he who sent me to you; he told me that Aulus found the master already dead yesterday morning."

Nissa's hands were pleating at her filthy tunic. "I could not understand it, no one seemed to know he was missing, there was no calling out of names and Assinius isn't here either. We all whispered to each other not to speak of either of them. I thought my son might have been sent out of the house on an errand that I didn't know about, or that . . ."

"Wait, you mean that Assinius wasn't in the house yesterday morning when the death was discovered?"

"Yes, my lord. I looked for him last night, no, it was the night before last, I suppose, after my lady had gone to bed. There was some message about the morning. He wasn't in the house and the porter didn't seem to know anything; he was very drunk, which isn't like him. He doesn't drink much even when he can get it because he's got a weak stomach."

"So Domina Faustina can't have known that the steward was not in the house, or she wouldn't have sent you to him. And there was no sign of him in the morning?"

"No, my lord. The guard just rounded us up and counted us and didn't seem to bother who we were. It was only the governor when we got here who made a fuss because there was no list of names."

"I told him I would mention that, but I won't! I suppose Domina Faustina thinks Assinius is here with the rest of you and is responsible enough to have provided what was wanted. Well, never mind, I can try to find him later. Nissa, how has it been? Have you all been questioned?"

"No, not all, and not since Aulus died. You knew about that?"

She had the rare quality of being able to cry quietly with the tears just running down her face but no sobs.

"Yes, I knew," said Camillus. "I suppose that was best for him."

"What god can tell that? While they had him, they were already working on the others. They took the housekeeper first"—she pointed to the fat woman still crying in the shadows at the back—"and a couple of the boys, but I suppose they didn't ask the right questions and then she started screaming and she hasn't really stopped since. It must have got on the guards' nerves and they saw they would never get any sense out of her. But that was yesterday afternoon, noble Tribune, and we haven't seen anyone except the guards since then. We thought it was all decided —I suppose we didn't know what to think."

"No, it's not decided, it can't be till after the games, didn't you know that? But you understand that Aulus's death hasn't helped at all. If he did it or they thought he did it, you must still all be punished."

"But we didn't, none of us. He'll have told you that?" She was very like her son; there was something of the same uncompromising quality about each of them. The gods knew they would both need it during the coming days. He drew her a step farther away from the other slaves.

"Nissa, do you know who killed your master?"

Something flared for a moment behind her eyes and then she put her hand to her mouth and tried to draw away from his hands on her shoulders. He could feel that she was trembling.

"What is it? You've remembered something and you must tell me. How else can I try to help you?"

"Noble Tribune, what can you do for us? Even if I could tell you a name now, what could you do? Oh, please, I'm grateful, of course I am. But the weight that's been laid on us, one man couldn't lift it alone. Hylas shouldn't have asked you."

The trouble was that she was probably right and he knew it, but that did not make it easier to accept hard truth from a slave woman. His hand tightened on her shoulder.

"Now, don't be silly. Leave me to decide what use can be made of any information you may have. I have a family too, you know, and we are not quite without influence."

She drooped in front of him then, the early frankness lost that the unexpected sight of him had surprised from her.

"Nissa," he whispered, "what is it? Think how your son is feeling now. How can he go free and leave you to die? And yet while he stays in the city he's in danger every hour.

I don't believe Aulus did it, I'm not going to denounce Hylas, but someone else will."

That got through, the thought of danger to Hylas. Really, the strength of a mother's love was extraordinary. She straightened up again and looked him in the eyes, and he could see that the new tears had made clean tracks down her dirty cheeks.

"Noble Tribune, I can't tell you who it could have been, but I do know that there were things that I thought were strange happening during the last few days. There was Assinius on that last evening before the dinner, I saw him talking to Decianus in the atrium. There shouldn't have been any reason for it except Assinius just being polite to a guest, but that wasn't how they were talking. It was as if this wasn't the first time and Decianus seemed very worked up but was trying not to show it."

"But you didn't hear even a word of what they were talking about?"

"No, nothing, I was too far away, but somehow I wasn't surprised when Assinius wasn't there the next morning when . . . when it happened."

Camillus thought that was going to be all and had taken his hand from her shoulder when she looked up again and said in a whisper, "I don't know, it's only a feeling this time, like you have when you've lost something and you know where you should look. Ask Merope, she doesn't miss much, and it may be that she could tell you what questions you should ask your wife."

VII

THE HOUSE OF DECIANUS

EVEN AFTER HE had left the prison and was walking again in the warm spring sunshine, Camillus could still feel the chill of it clinging to him. He had almost reached the Forum before he stopped to wonder where he was going and what he should do next. He had been lucky at the prison, but he had gone in unprepared and he could not risk doing that again, for his next visit must surely be to Domina Faustina at the Villa of the Galli.

The Forum was quiet, for the day was warm now and most citizens who were not at home eating were at the Circus. Camillus felt suddenly flat, tired, and worried. A dull, solid-sounding roar came from the direction of the Circus and a cloud of doves rose from the roofs of the colonnade opposite to flash and circle in the bright air. A chariot must have gone over on a turn, the crowd did not shout like that for a victory. Galerius would tell him later — when there was time to see Galerius again. For a moment he hated Hylas for asking for help, and Caius for getting himself killed, and even the miserable slaves for burdening him with their insoluble problem. Then he remembered the smell of the prison; he still felt dirty even after the chill had gone. What he needed was a bath and some food; he had not eaten since the night before. Camillus turned toward his favorite bathhouse.

After he had left his clothes, he went through the hot and cold rooms quickly; there was no one about that he knew well and he was left alone with his thoughts. He found an empty bench in the corner of the tepid room where he could stretch out and eat the sausages and small cakes a boy was hawking around. Now that his body was clean his mind was already beginning to work more clearly. He felt like a child fishing with a bent pin who draws in after a pull and finds that he has landed a whale. Hylas had turned to him with a confidence that had been touching at the time; he was aware of being at the edge of issues that he would certainly not be able to handle alone, but he could not involve anyone with the power to help until there was better evidence to go on than the distress of a few slaves and some unformed warnings of dread.

Later he must go home to give some account of his long absence. Nissa had spoken of Blandina, and at once his mind had closed with the thought that she could know nothing about her father's death. She had not even been in his house often since their marriage. He buried the thought of Blandina even deeper in his mind.

After an hour he got up, dived in at the deep end of the cold bath, swam a length, and got out. His thoughts were really no clearer, but his mind was rested and he could face Domina Faustina. In preparation for this he dressed with particular care.

The house where Decianus lived was in the quarter below the Gardens of Maecenas. It had been the property of a long-dead uncle who had made Decianus his heir; dark and high-roomed, it still felt more like a bequest than a home. Decianus's silent wife, Livonia, found it too much for her and lived almost entirely in the women's rooms at the back with her children.

Today more than ever, it was a house of mourning. The passage that led from the gate to the atrium yawned gloomily like an entrance to the underworld, and even the flittering ghosts were there, hopeful beggars who had heard the story in all its detail and were watching those who went in and out to see if they looked grieved or guilty.

Inside, it was even worse than Camillus had expected. He had hoped that the family would be alone in the hours before the funeral and that in quiet talk Domina Faustina might reveal to someone who was on the lookout a clue to what she was really feeling. But she was sitting enthroned in the atrium beside the open doors of the family shrine, still receiving the formal condolences of the clients of the dead man. By some act of generalship she had managed to bring with her from the stricken Villa Pomponia the family death masks that it was proper to display at such times, and all was arranged and ordered, with the table of offerings and smoking incense burner, as if she had been one of the great ladies of the Republic mourning for a Caesar or an Antony. By her side stood Decianus, stiff and tall, his horse face fallen into a mask as bleak and clay-colored as any ranged beside him.

The atrium was still half full of the small groups and single figures of the mourning reception, distant members of the family, colleagues, and neighbors. This is a mistake, thought Camillus. I must talk to her, but I can't do it here with all this coming and going, when all we do and say is as formal as a temple ritual. He had not seen her since the evening before the Ides, for when he had reached the Villa Pomponia on the morning of the murder she had already long left the house. This was not the place for a first meeting, it would be better to go now and come back after the funeral. Then the group in front of him turned to leave and he was face to face with the old woman and there was no chance to escape.

"Noble lady," he said, "can the respect and devotion of your family bring you any consolation in your loss? My wife is still prostrate with grief or she would have come herself, and I have scarcely been able to leave her since the terrible news reached us."

Domina Faustina turned down the corners of her mouth even more firmly. Clearly the dignity of being a Roman matron was supposed to take precedence over a daughter's grief. "So she will not be present at the funeral tonight?"

"That will hardly be possible. I can, of course, represent us both. It is unfortunate that my father is away from Rome. He will deeply regret that he cannot take this last opportunity to show respect to the head of a family to which he has so recently been allied by marriage."

"Respect and duty can be the only cure to grief," said Domina Faustina. "I shall find consolation in completing the ministrations that must be made on my family altar."

"My mother intends to supervise the necessary ritual herself for the remaining eight days of the funeral period," said Decianus.

"That will be a further ordeal," murmured Camillus. "I suppose that after tonight the house will be locked and empty, except for your mother's visits, though I imagine the prefect has placed a guard on it."

"Yes, in the circumstances my mother could not remain in it without her household and with Marcus away."

"My wife was greatly distressed when she heard that all

the family slaves had been arrested, and when she understood what their fate would be," said Camillus, lying flu-
ently. "Of course, she has known many of them since she
was a child and is concerned that the law punishes both
innocent and guilty together. I imagine that there can be no
hearing until the games are over, and perhaps by then some
way may be found to help them. Their value alone must be
a considerable part of the family estate."

"Innocent? There can be no question of innocence in a
case so clearly covered by the law," said Decianus. "As to
the value of the slaves, that cannot even be considered
when the law is so definite."

"They must die, the praetor will see to that," said Domina
Faustina in a quiet and final voice, folding her hands in her
lap.

Camillus was watching her closely. Was there something more hidden behind that always inscrutable mask of
a face? She had a look about her that in any other woman
would mean exhaustion, but of course Faustina could admit to no such human weakness. At least he had learned
one thing; the house was not going to be completely abandoned. It could be that the regular visits might be a cover
for someone searching for something that must be found.
For the first time he looked at Decianus closely and noticed
that a pulse in his forehead was twitching.

"So sudden a death is a tragedy at any time, but with
Marcus away and Caius Pomponius's secretary among the
condemned slaves I imagine you carry a very heavy burden
in settling the business affairs of the estate, sir," he said.

"My brother's papers were in good order. I expect few
difficulties," said Decianus, but Camillus noticed the pulse
move again.

"Will Marcus be sent for?" he asked.

"I think that would serve no useful purpose," said Decianus. "Everything would have been settled long before he could arrive, even if he took fast post horses."

"I should be glad to carry any messages when I go north at the end of the month."

Decianus blinked at that. He seemed to have forgotten that Camillus would see his nephew before anyone else in the family. *I wonder what he does not want me to tell Marcus,* thought Camillus.

Domina Faustina suddenly rose to her feet, and he noticed that the atrium was now empty of visitors. "The litters will be here soon. I must go and prepare myself. We expect to see you in an hour at the Villa Pomponia, Camillus Rufus."

She swept out. Decianus bowed to Camillus and followed her. An hour wasn't long; he would have to hurry.

As he walked quickly home, he considered what he had learned. Domina Faustina's feeling about the slaves seemed very clear, it was almost as if she were anxious for their deaths. The law would be allowed to take its course. But he was quite sure that they were both hiding something; neither of them thought that Aulus had killed his master, and it seemed likely that Decianus had already been through his brother's papers. But he was still no further forward in finding out what the quarrel had been about or what connection there was between Assinius and Decianus. It had not been the moment for asking any question as delicate as that.

Now he must tell Blandina some of what had happened and then attend the funeral, and all that time Hylas would be waiting for news of his mother. It would be some hours yet before he could get back to Matidia's room.

He was still living with his wife in his father's house. There had seemed no hurry about setting up a new home when he was due to rejoin his legion so soon and his father was absent in Syria.

Shouting to his valet, as he passed through the atrium, to put out his formal toga, he went up to the women's rooms. Blandina was curled up on a couch wearing a house robe, but she had done her face, and Merope was standing behind her combing the waves of dark hair that hung about her shoulders. Camillus just stopped himself in time from staring at the girl, trying to see in her face what it was that Nissa thought she might know. Blandina would certainly have misunderstood his motives, and Merope's face showed its usual careful blankness, unless you noticed the sharp black eyes that were missing nothing. Well, she must wait for the moment.

"My dear, where have you been all day?" Blandina asked, stretching up a hand to him as he bent to kiss her.

"Here and there in the city. I've just come from your uncle's house. You know the funeral is tonight?"

"Livonia was here this morning, she came with messages for you but I didn't know where to send them. I tried the houses of your friends, but they were all at the Circus."

"I'm sorry, I didn't mean to be so long." His boy had come in with the toga. Camillus gestured to him to wait while he sat down and began to comb his hair. He was hungry again, but food would have to be postponed until after the funeral; it would not be respectful to snatch a meal now.

"What did Livonia say apart from that?" he asked. "It seems such a strange business. Did Aulus suddenly go mad and kill your father? I don't see any other reason for anyone to do it unless he had enemies."

Blandina sat upright and twitched the comb away from Merope so that she could use it herself. "Who can question what the gods send? Perhaps it was Aulus suddenly going mad, or a houseboy with a grudge, or perhaps Father had enemies. He wasn't careful in what he said, you know, not careful as you have to be in Rome. All those years he was in Gaul when I was a child seem to have made him forget things. You can't drink toasts to Octavia at the moment— even if she is the Emperor Claudius's daughter and Nero's wife, she isn't in favor—but he did it at a dinner last month. He should know things like that. I do."

Camillus put down his own comb and turned to Blandina in amazement. "You don't think Aulus did it! Timon, stop fussing with that toga and get me a cup of wine."

Blandina, seeing the new look on his face, flicked her fingers at Merope, and the girl followed Timon out of the room.

"My dear Camillus, you look so tragic. My father is dead. I had feared for some time that he was in danger, but I could do very little about it. Of course I'm sorry that he was stabbed, didn't I cry all yesterday for him? But we are still alive and this business about the slaves is convenient, and I for one am not going to stir up trouble inquiring further. No one will remember the details in ten days' time, as things are, and the household wasn't worth all that much except for Merope and I'd taken her already."

"And you're content to leave it like that? Someone killed your father with a knife and you wouldn't lift a finger to have him brought to justice? I simply don't understand you!"

Camillus was standing up now, staring at his young wife in amazement, as if she were a stranger. The half-smile on her face did not change, but her eyes widened and seemed suddenly very dark. He was three years older, but he felt like an awkward boy before her.

"Camillus, what can I do? What could you do? These things happen. Perhaps I don't think Aulus did it, perhaps Grandmother doesn't either, but she remembers the days of Caligula, she can smell danger and I've learned to from her. Leave it, my dear, you can't do anything. If you say much more, I shall think you've got a girl among those slaves, and I shouldn't like that, not after less than a month."

Timon came back with the wine; Camillus drank it quickly, his face turned away from Blandina, and then stood with his arms out for the boy to drape the toga with its deep band of embroidery. It was the one he had worn for his marriage. That seemed an age ago now.

"It was fortunate Assinius was away from the house that night," he said over his shoulder. "I imagine that has saved his life. Do you know where he is, by the way?"

He turned to her then, and she was sitting straight up on the couch, and now the smile had faltered and there was fear behind the dark eyes.

VIII

THE FUNERAL OF CAIUS

THE BALCONIES THAT overlooked the Villa Pomponia were hung as thick with people as if one of the great state processions had been passing below. They were looking down into the peristyle where the funeral of Caius Pomponius was being prepared, and the body itself had just been brought from the bedroom to be arranged on the bier. It was the crowning moment.

Hylas, crouching on the floor between Varro's legs and the massive bulk of Aunt Matidia, was watching through a gap in the supports. From this angle he missed some things, but not the sight of his master's dead face, recognizable even from this height. As the swathed body was carried out by slaves belonging to Decianus and nervous hands fumbled at the awkward weight, the head fell back and the jaw moved as if he were still alive.

"Did you see that? The stiffness has worn right off," said Varro. "Well, it's nearly two days, high time it was over."

Hylas saw the dark shape of Faustina in her mourning robes come into his field of vision. With her own hands she arranged the head on the pillow, and propped the jaw into some semblance of decency with the heavy folds of the embroidered cover that had been arranged over the shrouded body. Hylas wondered who had washed it for burial, and who had arranged the room. Probably the bloodstained coverings were still there.

"There he is, there's young Camillus," said Matidia suddenly. Hylas wriggled, but could not see him.

It was a small procession, for it had not been thought fitting that the funeral masks should be carried by relatives before the bier, after the old custom, when the dead man had died so violent a death. Caius would have hated it, Hylas thought. He was always a man for display. Suddenly they were gone, the mourners, Domina Faustina in her carrying chair, and the small detail of guards who were to lead the way. Only Decianus's slaves were left, and as the watchers above turned away, they began the last tidying up. Matidia made a clucking sound of relief as a man carried a bundle from the master's bedroom; she was a practical soul.

"Stay there, will you, Auntie," said Varro. "We want to know who's left in the house."

Hylas crawled back into the room, keeping below the level of the balustrade. Inside, he could stand up and brush the dust and dead leaves off his knees.

"So he's gone," he said, looking at Varro. "I'm glad, thinking of him lying down there all these hours, after I'd seen how he looked . . . Well, I don't think they were right to take so long. Now I suppose we shall have to wait again. The tribune can't come for hours yet."

It was after dark when a heavy knock came, which rattled the beam in its socket. Instinctively Hylas drew back against the wall, although he now looked very different from the neat young secretary who might be on the guard's wanted list. Two days' growth of beard, some dirt, and the wreckage of one of Varro's market tunics had seen to that. The beam rattled again, and he threw himself down on Matidia's bed to sprawl like any unemployed young man who might have good reason to be there.

Varro went to the door and called through the latch hole. What he heard reassured him; he grinned back at Hylas and made a thumbs-up sign before sliding back the beam. Camillus came in quickly and the door was shut behind him.

Hylas came to his feet very fast with a look of trustful expectation that wrung Camillus's heart: there was so little that was hopeful to tell him.

"I'm sorry I was so long," he said. "What's happening now?"

"Just the usual clearing up. Is the guard still there, Auntie?" asked Hylas.

"Yes, dear, but the officer looks as if he's in a hurry. They'll be off soon."

Camillus sat down on the stool that Varro had set for him, but Hylas turned back toward the balcony, standing looking out at the pinkish glow that always hung over the close-set dark roofs of the city at night. His hand picked restlessly at the loose plaster by the door.

"I've seen your mother, I've seen everyone," said Camillus to his averted head. "Aulus is dead, the rest are alive, so far, and no one seems to know where Assinius is. He's certainly not with the others. I'm fairly sure Domina Faustina doesn't know this; she didn't know he hadn't been seen since the night before the murder. And you haven't been missed yet—or you hadn't been this morning. Everyone thinks someone else has given the governor a list of the slaves."

"Was it bad, in the prison?" Hylas asked.

"Not good, but your mother seemed well, and in command of things, and she hasn't been hurt." Hylas let out a deep breath but did not speak. Camillus went on: "You know, I believed you this morning when you said none of you had done it, but now I'm completely sure. Everything is pointing away from the slaves. And, Hylas, I've talked to the family, all of them, even my wife."

He paused for so long then that Hylas turned back to look at him. When he spoke again, his voice was very low. "Why, before the gods, did you bring me into this?"

It was almost dark in the room. Hylas could not see the young tribune's face and he was glad, for he too could now see the way the finger was pointing. "Someone killed my master because they were frightened of something he might do or say that would bring danger to others. That's right, isn't it? But I think it all happened very quickly and they made mistakes. Can't there be a reason behind that, some god who still cares for justice watching over the family, otherwise why was I allowed to escape? If I were in prison with the others, it would all be over now, except for young Marcus having to come back to it all. The senator would be buried and that would be the end of it. But it's not like that, I'm here, something made it possible for me to ask you for help. We can't escape from what is happening."

"Can't we? I'm sorry, Hylas, this is costing you far more than it ever can me. It's just the way my wife spoke—it's over, best forget about it. I was—shaken, I suppose. Don't worry, I didn't tell her about you. Now, what I keep asking myself is why did the murder happen then? Why that particular night?"

"It has to be something to do with the quarrel with

Decianus. Perhaps they were part of the same plan and Decianus thought my master had made a mistake."

"Think hard, Hylas, you said Aulus told you about it. Was there anything he heard, anything at all before Assinius pushed him out of the room?"

Hylas remembered the gray face in the warm kitchen glow. "Yes, he did say something, but I'm sure it wasn't enough to make sense. I remember, it was 'Even you can't have, we must have been mad.' "

" 'You can't have.' Something Caius Pomponius had done that his brother thought was crazy or dangerous. But 'we must have been mad.' not just 'I.' And, Hylas, didn't you say that before dinner your master seemed to have lost some papers?"

"Yes, I was surprised, because he was always a bit careless about his correspondence, so I looked after all his papers. I'd never known him to have anything secret before. I couldn't understand at the time why he didn't explain what was missing."

Something slipped into place in Camillus's mind, something Blandina had said earlier in the evening about her father and his lack of political sense. Could the senator have been mad enough to be part of a conspiracy, and been killed when he was found to be too dangerous? But who had used the knife—another conspirator or a member of the family?

"I think he was looking for a quite small scroll," Camillus said aloud. "Probably one that looks like something else and must have been picked up by mistake. I think there may be names on it, and they will tell us the 'why' of this murder and probably the 'who' too. And there are so few people to choose from. I think you already understand that as clearly as I do."

There was very little light coming from the brazier by now. Camillus looked across at the dark shape of Varro. "Could we have a lamp?"

Varro lit one and put it down where the glow shone on the faces of both the young men. "Noble Tribune, you've made it hard for him, you know, saying that. It's clear enough that one of the family killed the senator to keep them all out of trouble, and anyone can see the mess that puts you in, being married to the daughter. But you can't expect a lad like Hylas to stand up and say, 'Yes, my mistress murdered my master.' How can he prove it? You know they take evidence from slaves only under torture, and how's he to know you won't turn on him when he's said it?"

It was as tense in the little room as if a storm were coming. Camillus stood up wearily. The little man was right, of course. He would always have to carry the weight himself, take the decisions, and say what had to be said; what else could he expect? He felt he had aged a year already since he had looked at his wife earlier in the evening and seen her properly for the first time, and begun to understand what fear could do even inside a family. Hylas had risen too, automatically. Camillus put out a hand to him, half helpless, half reassuring, and they both sat down again. Unexpectedly, it was Hylas who spoke first.

"Varro, you shouldn't have spoken to the tribune like that. How does one ever know one can trust anyone, how did I know I could trust you? You either do or you don't. You think it was Domina Faustina, don't you, sir? Perhaps she didn't stick the knife in, herself, someone else may have done that. But she saw the danger and did what she had to do."

Camillus felt as if he had suddenly been given perhaps the most valuable gift one man can give another, but it was something fragile and not to be spoken of.

"Wait a minute," he said, keeping his voice practical and businesslike. "You're right, of course, and I knew we were both thinking this way even this morning when we first spoke. But if the list, or whatever it was, was missing, hadn't she taken it, and if so, where was the danger?"

"What if she didn't take it, what if she only knew it was missing?"

"Then judging by how she looked today, she still thinks it's missing, and what chance has she had to search the villa for it? She may have been looking during the night before the murder when Matidia saw her, but she wouldn't have killed Caius if she had been successful. In the morning there was no time, and since then she's been here only for the funeral."

"Decianus Gallus must have looked as well. He was in the plot, too, he must have been, and he's had the best chance when he came to make the arrangements. He was the one Madam loved and would have tried to save. Caius was only her stepson."

The last piece clicked into place. "It fits, then, doesn't it? Even that Domina Faustina told me that she would be coming to the house every day during the mourning period to make the offerings. Then she can search at her leisure; she knows Decianus hasn't found anything, so it's her turn, and if she finds that paper before we do, then our last chance has gone. We need to get into the house tonight."

Camillus began to consider the possibilities. Would it be

possible for him to trick the guards into letting him in, or was there some other way that Hylas had overlooked when he escaped? He was surprised when the slave stood up suddenly.

Hylas looked down at him, feeling sick and very cold. He hoped that it did not show how much he was trembling even though he had wrapped his arms tightly around his body. Camillus saw and understood.

"Hylas, do you think you can?" he asked quietly. It was the only hope, but he would never have been able to ask.

Varro spoke from the darkness. "I could go down, sir. I'm better at ropes than Hylas."

"But would you know what to look for and where to look?" asked Hylas in a flat voice. "I was born in that house, I know every stone of it. I don't know if I can, but I'll try. I know there isn't anyone else. But we must wait, mustn't we? It's too early yet."

He sat down on the bed again. Camillus left him alone to deal with the mixed blessings of a strong imagination and went out to stand beside Matidia and look into the darkened house below.

"They've all gone," said the old woman. "And the slaves helped themselves to this and that from the kitchen. Someone forgot to lock up properly!"

"Has the guard been set yet?" he asked.

"There's no one inside the house—I counted them in and out—but the centurion had a look around not long ago."

"Could you get a message sent to my wife?" Camillus asked Varro. "I must stay here tonight now."

"I could do it, noble Tribune, but is it safe for you here?" Varro dropped his voice so that Hylas inside the room could not hear what he was saying. "If things should go wrong and he's taken, he knows what will happen and he's sweating over it now. He'll be lucky if they kill him quickly. But if that should happen, they'll search the block, and if you're found it would be bad for you and bad for all of us. The less there is to connect you with here the better. We'll be all right. There's nothing to show Hylas was ever here, and he'll try not to tell, poor lad. But you . . . no, I don't like it. You're much better on your way home soon, if you'll excuse me saying so. I'll get word to you early in the morning."

"You may be right, but I don't like going away and leaving him now, with that ahead of him."

Camillus saw the man's teeth flash in the faint light as he smiled. "He's better off just with us, sir. It's a bit of a strain being brave in front of someone you respect, and he'll mind what you think more than he minds us."

"You know what I think."

"Yes, but it wouldn't help to say so. You'll be in some tight spots in your army days, sometime. You know what the old hands say: make the dangerous job seem normal and nothing to fuss about and the recruits won't have the sense to know otherwise."

"I see. All right, I'll go, but send him down before midnight. The guard will be changed then, and he should go in when they're sleepy."

"I'll go out and past the house with you, so we can see how things are," said Varro.

He came back alone half an hour later in an optimistic frame of mind. The front gate of the villa was fastened with a large chain. It would take some time to undo even if anyone heard a sound from inside the house, and there were only two guards, both at the front. One of them was on his feet and keeping a proper watch while the other was dozing against the wall. Varro thought that the centurion on duty at the market would probably make his rounds from time to time, but no one would go through that door without a very good reason. Also, it was a cloudy night and there was only a new moon. It would be dark as the mouth of Hades soon.

Matidia had come in from the balcony when it was too dark to see anything, and now she was pottering around, getting a meal. Some of the things she put in the soup were unusual mixtures of scraps that Varro had brought down from the market and her stock of potherbs. However, it smelled good, and Hylas knew he would have wolfed it down eagerly enough if his stomach had not been screwed into a tight knot inside him. All he wanted was water to drink, and not much of that. He was more scared than he had ever been in his life, and there were at least two hours to think about it before he could actually do anything.

Before they had finished eating, there was another knock on the door. Varro looked up. "He's never come back so soon!"

A voice shouted outside.

"No, dear, that's Vibulanus from upstairs. His wife must be bad again. He'll shout till I let him in."

"Right," said Varro. "Sit tight, Hylas, and don't talk. You may look pretty rough but you don't sound it."

Hylas lounged back on the bed, holding his almost untouched bowl of soup. He was eating noisily as Varro let in a fat man in a filthy, bloodstained tunic.

"My mate Titus," Varro said, with a nod over his shoulder at Hylas. "It's all right, Vibulanus isn't the public executioner, he works at the butcher's down the street. What is it, the same trouble as last time?"

"If I've told her once that pork's poison to her unless she takes it down to the baker's to be roasted properly, I've told her a thousand times. But what do I find? Her cutting collops off the joint and charring them over the stove because she's too idle to go down the stairs twice. Now she's lying there yelling as if she was having triplets. Can you give me something for a purge, Matidia?"

"Quick-acting or slow?" asked Matidia, getting up and rummaging in the shadows among her bundles.

"Quick, if I'm to get an hour of sleep tonight."

"Here you are, dear. It's a powder. As much as will cover your thumbnail in half a cup of wine and water. And I'd be grateful for a bit of tripe next time you've got some handy."

Vibulanus looked as if he would have been glad to stay longer, leaning against the door, but a shrill voice shouted down the stairs outside.

"Dad, be quick, she's ever so bad."

The man sighed and rolled his eyes upward. "What a night we shall have," he complained, and slouched off.

"He won't be down again, he won't have time," said Matidia, with a cackle. "That was squirting cucumber root I gave him. She won't eat pork again in years."

"He'll know me if he sees me again," said Hylas, putting down his bowl.

"Don't worry, son," said Matidia. "He stares at everyone, he's just ignorant, it didn't mean anything. We often have Varro's friends here."

"Well, I must remember my name's Titus if anyone else comes," said Hylas. "Varro, have you got a rope?"

Varro had, a twisted rawhide that he knotted at regular intervals so that Hylas could get a better grip. They took it out and fastened it firmly to the balustrade; it was long enough to reach down to the roof, as far as they could tell. Slowly the clatter through the thin walls from the neighbors faded into the background hum of a great city that is never quiet. There was still the racket of carts passing the end of the road on the way to the market, for no wheeled traffic was allowed in the narrow streets during the day.

Hylas stood up at last and looked around him. His satchel and tunic had been stowed out of sight; now he got them out again and packed everything that he had brought with him tidily together. Last of all, his sandals.

"There, if you need to get rid of it quickly, that's everything," he said. "If I don't get out again, it should sell for a little, and you'll be welcome."

Varro did not argue. He was a practical man and knew the dangers ahead well enough, and the times when a man could be saved by a few coins in his belt.

"Yes, you're better barefoot," was all he said. "It'll be easier to grip. What about a lamp?"

"There are lamps in every room once I'm down there, and if Domina Faustina has put out the offering table in the atrium there'll be something burning there to light one from. I'm off now, I can't wait any longer."

He went over to Matidia and gave her a hug, but could not think of anything to say. Varro followed him out onto the balcony.

"I'm sorry I'm not heavy enough to give you a proper

pull up if you need one in a hurry. But it's best not to get anyone else in. The neighbors aren't all like Vibulanus, but there isn't one I'd trust with this. Do you know where to look?"

"Yes and no. It's not anywhere easy, but I can't think properly up here. Varro, if you hear anything, if anything goes wrong, pull the rope up at once. I won't be able to get out with the guard after me — I could never climb the rope. It's bad enough when I can take my time, and there's no need to lead the guard straight here."

Varro gripped him hard but did not answer. He picked up the coiled rope and began to let it down flat against the wall like a careful snake. It hardly showed in the shadow, for the night was so dark now that they could barely make out each other's faces. Hylas hitched up his tunic and dried his sweating hands on the seat. Then he got a leg over the balustrade.

IX

THE VILLA AT NIGHT

THE FIRST FEW feet were the worst even though there was more to hold on to. Once he was below the level of the balcony, alone and out of Varro's reach to help, his heart stopped thumping. There was no time now to remember why he had volunteered so meekly to do it, or whom it was for, only that there was a task to do that needed every muscle of his untrained body and every scrap of his endurance. He must think no further ahead than that.

His hands slipped on the rope and he slid a few feet, but found a toe hold to bring him up before he clattered down onto the tiles below. Now he was so far down, the courtyard was not completely dark. That puzzled him until he reached the roof itself and could see the faint glow coming from the atrium. That would be Faustina's table of offerings, of course. He worked his way around to the skylight into the attic without slipping on the mossy tiles, and let himself down into the dusty silence inside. When he had reached the upper gallery he stood panting hard, safe from the sight of anyone not directly opposite him, and began to think that now there was just a chance he might get out of the house a second time alive. All evening he had not got as far ahead as that, only to the effort of will that would make him start something that seemed impossible because there was nothing else he could do, like a soldier caught in a helpless last stand.

He stood very still, hearing the house at night, listening for any sound, any breath that might warn him of danger, of another living being in the house—Matidia could have been mistaken.

Hylas walked down the stairs with his bare feet cold and silent on the stone steps. He must face the worst first, the most sensible place for his master to keep anything of value, the room on the west side with its stripped bed and the water still lying in the cracks in the mosaic floor. He found a lamp where he had expected, in a niche at the foot of the stairs. It was a little pottery thing that would fit into the palm of his hand and give no more than a bead of light with the wick pulled down. He stood again to listen, behind the curtains half drawn across the entrance to the atrium. From here he could look past the table beside the fish tank, with its small stone altar, the incense burner, and the ornamental vases, lit by a tiny lamp. Cracks of light showed around the double doors that closed the outer gateway, and a shadow passed them. The guards were still awake.

The shrine would have been enough to scare him even in daylight, with friends at his back, for Faustina had carried home the masks that had been displayed in the house of Decianus, and they were ranged in the open doors of the great oak cupboard, looking, with their shadowed eye sockets, not alive but very much aware, like spectators in a box at the Circus. As the lamp flickered in the night air and shadows jumped, it was all he could do to light the lamp and get back to the peristyle without running from their malevolent gaze.

The master's room still smelled bad. Hylas had not

realized that the taint of blood could hang in the air so long. He saw at once that the chest that was usually locked had been emptied of its contents, for it was open and the top had been left leaning back against the wall. He held the lamp high; where else was there to look? All the small valuable things in the room had been taken, the Corinthian vase, the ivory box that held the master's toilet set. Someone had been through it thoroughly.

He was glad to let the curtain fall back behind him and to go next door into the familiar presence of his library, but even here someone had been ahead of him. The two hangings at either end of the room had been wrenched down from their hooks, and the door of the book cupboard was open. At the sight of that, Hylas began to hate Decianus, if that was who it had been, in a more personal way. Much of this belonged to Marcus now; what right had that man to come to search, to damage and to throw aside? He put the lamp down on the end of the writing table and began to sort and rearrange the scrolls automatically, putting them back in their boxes. It had to be done if he was to be sure that an unexpected scroll or small tablet had not been slipped in among them and missed earlier, and the handling of familiar things comforted him.

He had to admit at last that there was nothing there. Sitting down on his stool, he looked around the room; upstairs with Varro he had not thought as far as this. He had said that he knew every stone in the house, and that was true enough if it meant that he knew the places where it would be useless to look. There were chests and shelves and stores that other members of the household went to every day; no one would have dreamed of hiding anything there.

Then he was unexpectedly hungry. It was certainly hours since he had eaten more than a mouthful of soup. While he was thinking he might as well eat, and from what Matidia had said there must still be food in the house. Shielding the tiny lamp with his hand, he crossed the peristyle again and went down into the kitchen. The shadows shooting across the wall produced a low buzzing sound like a sleepy beehive that startled him until he raised the flame higher and saw the gaping ribs of the sucking pig that had been the main course of the dinner. The cook would have covered it, but the greedy slaves who had washed the body must have pulled the cover aside in their search for pickings. Now the flies had got to it and the air stank sweet; the gaping ribs pulled away from the backbone looked uncomfortably like the small corpse from an old tragedy.

Hylas looked around him for something more wholesome to eat. He found a bowl of nuts, some stale bread left over from the day before and half a cheese kicked under the cook's chopping block; there was nothing else. He even opened the door of the bread oven built into the thickness of the outer wall, but he found only the charred and shriveled remains of the loaves that had been newly set to bake before the dawn when Aulus had stumbled into the atrium with his bloodstained hand. The cook who should have turned them and minded the fire had been led away with the other slaves, and it had roared itself out uselessly, spoiling the bread, as so much else had already been spoiled in that house.

He took the bread and cheese out where the air was fresher and sat down on a step to eat. Once he looked up at the balcony, four floors above him, but it was lost in the general blackness of the side wall of the insula. Varro would still be there, straining his eyes down into the darkness below, but he would see nothing even if Hylas waved, only perhaps the prick of flame from his lamp as Hylas moved backward and forward.

But where was he to move next? He could go back and tell Varro first and then Camillus tomorrow that there was nothing there; he had looked but found nothing. Hylas stood up and nearly went back up the stairs. Then he sat down again. All he had done so far, Varro could perfectly easily have done for him, as he had offered. He began to go methodically around the rooms in his mind; it was no help. There might be a dozen cupboards hidden in the walls or loose paving stones that he would never find. It had to be somewhere where even the master of the house would not think to look, and somewhere easy to get at quickly.

First he tried the dining room. There was not much chance that papers had been hidden under the mattresses, but Hylas looked all the same, and also behind and inside the carved cupboard where the dinner cups and best wine service were stored. There might be a secret hiding place there, and he searched carefully, but all he found was a few spiders.

He sat back on his heels, and it was then that the first flicker of understanding came into his mind. It was simple, suddenly, and when he knew where to look for the scroll he thought he knew who had hidden it, although it made no sense. He had remembered, for the first time since it happened, Blandina boasting of making her offering to the family gods. He walked quickly through into the atrium and over to the shrine. If there was anything that was not already in the hands of Decianus or Faustina, then it was here. He put his small lamp down on the offering table, wiped his sweating hands again on his tunic, and began to move the row of plaster masks very carefully one by one, laying them down on the floor in the same order. He was almost sobbing under his breath now; his heart was racing at the horror of what he was doing, for his master would have had any slave flogged almost to death for touching these, the most sacred things in the house. The Stoic philosophy he had taken in along with his education gave him no protection from the fears he had now.

With the grinning faces staring up at him in a double row from the floor he could peer at last into the shadowy corners at the back of the shrine. There were many things there, nameless bundles, ancient smoke-blackened figurines treasured by many generations of the house of the Pomponii who had gone before. He recognized the tarnished gold-ball charm that Marcus had worn around his neck when he was a child and that had been dedicated there when he had come of age.

Very delicately, moving the lamp in the low space between the shelves, he felt here and there among the dusty treasures. It must be here and yet he could not find it. His fingers were sweating again and growing clumsy. A little figure slipped and fell, knocking its head off against a lower shelf, but he dived for the body and caught it before it hit the ground. Crouching low like that, and listening above the sound of his heart for any noise from outside that would show the chinking had been heard, he rested his face against the smooth, age-darkened wood of the shrine, and looking up, he saw it.

Tucked neatly between the supports of the upper shelf was a narrow scroll sealed with a cord. No one standing before the shrine would ever see it, for it was well below eye level, and even if one were kneeling and looking straight in to the lower shelves, it was hidden by the carved moldings along their front edges. Reverently Hylas set the little broken goddess back in the darkest corner he could find, and then eased the paper out of its hiding place. It was not tied and he knew the handwriting at once. It was a list of names and the second was Decianus Gallus. Hylas did not look further; what he held in his hand could have extinguished the houses of both the Pomponii and the Galli if it had come to light during a search after an unsuccessful plot. The families must have learned that the list existed; Caius's death came from that one fact alone. The rest Camillus would untangle in the morning. Now he had to put the shrine to rights, conceal all signs of his visit, and somehow climb that terrible rope again.

When the last of the masks was in place, Hylas felt a little better. He was sure as he stepped back to get a better look that no one would have known they had been moved, but that was when his hand caught the edge of the offering table, rocking it back on its bronze claw feet. A slim alabaster vase holding incense fell over and clattered against the lamp.

Hylas swooped down for the precious scroll lying at his feet, and at the same time his hand closed over his own small lamp, snuffing the flame but knocking it to one side under the legs of the table. He froze still, his eyes fixed on the faint lines of light around the gates, and his ears straining to hear a pause in the regular footfalls of the guards. But the noise he heard came from a different place, a thunderous yawn from the porter's cubbyhole beside the gates and inside the house.

He dived across to the concealing shadows of the archway into the peristyle like a startled bat. He had been in the house an hour and not thought to listen at the one door behind which any watcher was certain to be. Not one of the guard, but some man left behind by Decianus who would never have come through into the peristyle to be seen by Matidia. There was no time to wait to make sure. He stuffed the paper down the front of his tunic, and hitched his belt tighter as he fled up the stairs toward the attic. Only when he was actually up on the roof did he pause to look down over the stone parapet. A larger lamp was moving in the atrium. A quick search made by a sleepy man among the shadows might show nothing except an unsteady vase that could have fallen over on its own, unless his own lamp was spilling oil at the feet of the searcher.

The light was carried out into the peristyle and held high. Hylas had a glimpse of an unfamiliar face as the man looked around him, clearly none too willing to search the house alone; he went back into the atrium.

Hylas did not wait to see if he was going to call the guard. His eyes were used to the dark and he scrambled across the roof like an accomplished burglar. The comforting line of the rope hung above him and he heard a faint hiss. Varro was still there. Hylas tried to close his mind again to everything except the next handhold, the next crack in the crumbling face of the wall. When he had got his knee up on the projecting beam he stopped to listen. There were voices below in the house, but they were some way away. He nearly fell then, but Varro was reaching far down with both arms, and from the muttering he could hear above, Matidia had Varro by the waist. Hylas felt the hard edge take the skin off his already bruised ribs as he was hauled over the balustrade for the second time to land on the floor of the balcony.

"I got it!" he hissed, making even a whisper seem triumphant.

"And they'll get you if we stay here." Varro dragged him into the room. "Look, Auntie, we must be off. I'll see you in the morning, but they could be up here before we finish if we stop to hear the story. I don't know what the lad found, but he must have been noisy about it!"

"I won't ask you where you're going, dear," said Matidia, seemingly not the least disturbed. "Don't forget the rope, that would make them think!"

Varro whisked it in from the balcony and began to coil it around his body under his tunic. "Carry this," he said to Hylas, pushing a dirty sack into his arms. Hylas felt the edges of his satchel inside and grinned.

"Where to?"

"You'll know if we get there!"

X

THRASEA PAETUS

CAMILLUS HAD LAIN awake in the dark until the third hour after midnight, hearing the regular breathing of his wife, but conscious only of each difficult and dangerous step that Hylas might be taking. He had cursed Varro on the way home for persuading him to go away, and yet the man had been right; all semblance of unconcern in his behavior would have gone if he was unexpectedly away from home all night. Already his wife was furious with him that he would not tell her where he had spent the day.

He had meant to be up before dawn and at the insula as soon as it was safe to be in the streets, but it was a dark morning with low cloud and spitting rain and his valet overslept too. When Timon did come in, contrite and clumsy, he woke too fast, heavy-eyed, and as he dressed quickly, he had to take comfort from knowing that one way or another Hylas must by now have done what he could.

As he stood by his bed cramming down two mouthfuls of bread, while the slaves outside clattered pails in the atrium and made the usual muddle of the morning cleaning, his father's porter came trotting through from the front door and called up to Timon.

"He says there are two gentlemen to see you, my lord, noble senators," said the boy.

"Why does he never bother to ask people's names?" said

Camillus crossly. Still chewing the last mouthful of his breakfast, he hurried down the stairs and nearly choked when he found himself confronted by one of the most unwelcome faces in Rome.

Decianus stood awkwardly, with the angles of his bony body and his large hands somehow at odds with the folds of his toga; behind him stood another, much older man, thin and dignified: Thrasea Paetus, former consul and one of the most respected men in Rome, Camillus' father's friend. He blushed as he tried to compose himself and greet such a distinguished guest at the same time.

"Gentlemen, this is an early honor you pay me," he said, playing for time. Suddenly he saw a small but ugly picture in his mind of Hylas, broken already by hours of torture, confessing all their plans and suspicions and implicating him in some undreamed-of treason. Could this be the polite prelude to an arrest? He glanced through to the atrium, but there were no guards waiting, and yet he could think of no good reason Decianus could have had for visiting him unless he was getting suspicious. Thrasea Paetus's presence was a complete mystery.

"My dear Camillus," said Decianus, coming forward, "we were deeply touched yesterday by the solicitude you showed to our bereaved family. The funeral is now well over, we thank the gods, although my mother remains inconsolable."

"It will be a bitter blow to Marcus Pomponius, so far away," said Camillus, still speaking formally. "When bad news comes already many days old, when one is cut off from the familiar observances, it is hard to bear."

"You will be wondering why I am here, Camillus Rufus," said the older man. "The truth is that when I went to the house of Decianus Gallus to pay my respects this morning, he spoke of the comfort you had been to the family in their tragic loss. But it seemed to us hard that the remainder of your leave should be completely clouded by it, and I was reminded of the invitation I had made to you on the day before the Ides."

Camillus's amazement must have shown in his face at the invitation being repeated now. He started to say, "But, noble Senator, the period of mourning . . ."

"Exactly. It would be most unsuitable for you to be seen in the public seats with your usual companions, but it so happens, as I told you before, that I must attend the praetor who is president of the games. If you would come with me, I should be glad of your company and it would help me to perform what is an irksome social duty without disgracing myself completely. I know little about the affairs of the Circus." At the surprise that still showed in Camillus's face, the senator's grave expression relaxed into an unexpectedly understanding smile. "Oh dear, I can see I must still appear to you like an ancient uncle offering a sad child a sweet, but I had hoped both to provide myself with a guide and to give you a not unwelcome diversion."

"Senator," said Camillus, "you must think I've lost my manners completely. You are offering me a chance any young man in Rome would be glad of, so what can I say except that you are doing me too great an honor."

"Good, then that is settled, and I am only glad that Decianus brought it back into my mind. However, I am on my way to the Circus now, and you, as I can see, have not quite completed your toilet."

Camillus saw the senator's eyes take in his house slippers and uncombed hair. He directed the visitors toward the most sheltered corner of the atrium and hurried back up to his own room. As he stood impatiently while Timon arranged his toga, their voices outside floated up to him.

"The slaves, of course, are a cause for concern. It is most unfortunate that the Festival of Ceres will delay the inquiry into the murder." That was Thrasea Paetus.

Then Decianus came in, bland and high-pitched. "Oh, no, my dear Senator, I had it from the praetor late last night that the matter might be advanced. It seems that the Emperor has already been made familiar with the case and may authorize an earlier inquiry. As it is, April 20 is a most inconvenient day; even if the business can be hurried through, it does not give time for the sentences to be carried out. It would be most inauspicious to celebrate the birthday feast of Rome next day with the execution of slaves."

"So you think an advance is likely?"

"Who can say? But we are convinced of the slaves' guilt and would be glad to have the matter settled. The strain on my mother is very great."

Timon was trying to tell him something, but he turned away, not wanting either the boy or Blandina, sitting up in bed and combing her hair, to see his face. So the invitation had been a trap, and Decianus had snapped it shut neatly behind him. Someone had decided that his interest in the slaves was a nuisance, someone who might have heard by now that he had been to the prison. Someone had had the influence to exploit the good will of Thrasea Paetus mentioned in casual conversation, so that the invitation was not really a request but a command. And someone was here to make sure that it worked and that he had no chance of further mischief before he was safely shut in the Circus for the day. A lot could happen while he was there, unable to speak to anyone or do anything, and a refusal now would be inexcusably rude and impossible to explain.

Already the small warning pulse that Caius seemed to have lacked, and which all men in public life needed to warn them of danger, was beginning to beat. Hylas would be waiting for him at the insula, the key to the murder might be waiting in Matidia's room to be put into his hands, but if he did not go to the Circus there would be danger. If he was out of favor, he could help no one, and he must consider the risk to his own family.

Timon was still standing there, looking puzzled. He took him by the shoulders and led him over to the door. "Now listen, and listen well. This must be done at once and there must be no gossiping about it or you will be in painful trouble!"

He gave exact instructions as to how Matidia's room could be reached and made the boy repeat them back. "When you get there, tell whoever you find, it may be an old woman or a young man with dark hair, that you come from me and that the senator Thrasea Paetus has taken me with him to the Circus; then bring back any message they send. Tell whoever is there that Varro should come to me after the seventh hour."

There was no more time, he could not keep Thrasea Paetus waiting any longer, but there was still Blandina.

"What is going on?" she asked, opening her eyes very wide, in a way he was just beginning to distrust.

"I'm being taken to the Circus like a good child. Your uncle thought I might like it. How kind of him!"

"Well, I did say something last night about how dull it is

for you, with the funeral and everything while the festival is on."

"Last night? Who to?" He stopped short in the doorway and turned back to her, with a cold, intent look on his face that she had never seen before.

"Camillus, stop it, I'm not a sentry you're interrogating! Didn't I mention it? I went round to be with Aunt Livonia during the funeral. Why shouldn't I? You'd left me alone all day."

"And what else did Aunt Livonia say? What else have you arranged for me?"

"Nothing, don't be so silly. I wasn't to know that Thrasea Paetus was going to come this morning, was I?"

Merope had come into the room with her mistress's breakfast and had been listening to their conversation far more obviously than well-trained slaves usually did.

"My lady, tell the master about Assinius. That was strange, wasn't it?" she said suddenly. Blandina shot her a look that would have meant trouble for anyone who could not look after herself, but Merope usually could. Since she was exceptionally good at dressing hair, her mistress did not bully her as much as she did the other slaves.

"What about Assinius?"

"Oh, it was some nonsense about his being missing, but I didn't take much notice. After all, he might not have been in the house when Father was killed, so it can't be anything to do with that."

Camillus suddenly remembered the men waiting outside. "I regret that I shall have to leave you again for most of the day," he said. "But I shall expect all the family news when I get back."

As he walked quickly through the colonnade that led to the atrium, he heard a flutter behind and found that Merope had followed him. Now the usual confidence had gone from her small painted face, and she looked young and frightened.

"Please, noble Tribune, please," she whispered.

"Merope, this evening. I've no time now," he said, trying not to sound too impatient.

"But can you tell me, they will all be killed, all the household?"

"I'm afraid so, unless someone can find another murderer, and there's not much time for that."

"All of them, Nissa and . . . and Hylas? He was valuable."

Camillus cursed inwardly as he felt the blood rise quickly into his face. She saw it at once. "So you do know. I was sure you did. He escaped, didn't he, like Assinius?"

There was no point in denying it. "How did you know that? Merope, if you breathe a word of this to anyone, I'll hand you over to the authorities along with the others. You've not been out of the household long."

"It was something about a list, I heard my mistress talking last night, and Hylas not being on it. I guessed then, but I've seen Assinius."

"Where? You can't have!"

"I'm sure it was he, but he's shaved his beard off and he was wearing a very expensive new cloak. It was when we were leaving the Villa Gallia last night. He came out of the alley down beside the house that leads to the side door, but he ducked back when he saw us."

"If anyone in the household was ever kind to you and you wish them well, don't speak about what you've told me to anyone, it could be important. Go quickly now, or your mistress will wonder what we're talking about."

Merope flashed him a glance of complete understanding and disappeared back up the stairs.

As he joined the two men waiting in the atrium, his mind was churning and he felt sick. Too much was happening and there was no time to sort it out or try to understand it. And now he would have to make polite conversation all the way to the Circus as if he had no care in the world. He could see by the smug look on Decianus's face as he left them in the street outside that he was congratulating himself on having done something clever. Well, all was not lost yet.

Not very far away, in the storeroom of a shop opposite the market, Hylas sat on a sack of what felt like dried fish heads and wondered that he had ever thought Matidia's room smelled strange. In front of him two crusted bronze caldrons steamed while a small boy crouching between them blew up the smoldering charcoal with a goatskin bellows. The shop sold sauces and relishes of the cheapest kind to the many cookshops and eating places clustered near the market. Curled back in his corner, Hylas put his head down and shut his eyes. He was very tired, and though sleep seemed impossible, between the racket of the market and the smell of boiling vinegar that made his eyes smart, at least he could rest in what seemed perfect safety. Of all the places where the guard might be looking for him, this was one of the most unlikely for an escaping secretary.

Varro had hurried him out of Matidia's room and from the block itself by an indirect route down a back staircase and some alleys so narrow that he could barely squeeze through. It was not until Hylas had been safely hidden in the storeroom that there had been time to say what had happened.

"I'll go back at dawn," said Varro. "I daren't leave you till then. Auntie will manage all right, but they're sure to search the block and the tribune could walk right into it."

Then, as Hylas fished in the sack to bring out the scroll, he laid a quick hand on his arm. "No, not here, we know there's death in it. I don't need to know what sort. Besides, people who've never seen papers can't describe them to anyone who's asking. Patience, the tribune will sort it out."

Hylas opened a sleepy eye. The sun was well up, and Varro had been gone two hours now. What could be wrong this time? Always the hope of safety seemed to be moving away from him, further away all the time. First he had only wanted to escape from the house, then to have the scroll safely, then to be in a sure hiding place. Now—to have Camillus tell him in his firm voice what should be done. But how was he to tell the tribune that he was almost certain that it was Blandina who had hidden the scroll? What help would Camillus give him then? Now, hidden here, he was almost as much a prisoner as the other slaves, for without Varro he could not leave his hiding place. Time goes slowly when one is frightened.

XI

THE CIRCUS MAXIMUS

THE SUN SHINING straight down the length of the Circus Maximus half-blinded Camillus as he followed Thrasea Paetus into the marble splendors of the president's box. The first race was already over, and the triple tiers of seats seemed solid with faces as far along as he could see clearly. There was a great roar of noise, the arguments of two hundred thousand fervent supporters of the different factions who had either won or lost bets on the race. The box was furnished with carved chairs for the president and the more important guests in front, and an assortment of padded couches and marble tables farther back under the shade of the crimson canopy. It might be warm later if the wind dropped; the early drizzle had cleared, but at the moment the air was still cool, and the canopy strained at its golden cords and flapped and cracked like a sail at sea.

The praetor, in deep conversation with one of the senior stewards of the Circus, broke off to greet them and wave vaguely to empty seats where they could look down on the row of starting gates let into the colonnade below. As the noise was too great to make further conversation easy, Camillus was able at last to think his very uncomfortable thoughts in peace.

Decianus wanted him stopped from doing further mischief and this was for him the most perfect prison in

Rome—he could neither speak nor refuse to speak nor even write a letter without half the Senate in their seats away to his right, and everyone else within two hundred paces, being aware of it. And while he sat here, thirteen slaves might be hurried away to an unjust death, and a brave young man be facing implacable cruelty. He decided two things at once: that nothing he could do would make it possible for him to escape before noon, but that after that, even if he had to fake a fit, he must get home somehow to see what message the boy had been able to bring him from Matidia. The news that he was going to the Circus must have made the others think he had abandoned them, but again there was nothing he could do about that for the moment.

Also there were the races themselves, and he was a normal young man who could not sit for some hours in the best seats in the Circus without having his interest aroused in any way. The imperial box halfway down the eastern side was still empty, but preparations were now beginning for the next race. From below he could hear the horses and the grating of chariot wheels pulled forward and back in the confined space behind the starting rope, and there was the usual confusion of ostlers, grooms, and hangers-on that horses seem to collect about them, controlled by the permanent staff of the Circus and the detachment of city guard on crowd duty.

"You, I imagine, are a Greens man," said Thrasea Paetus with a smile, making an attempt to speak pleasantly about something he did not understand.

Camillus, indeed a Greens man since he was at school, found himself saying, "Oh, no. My father always supported the Whites after a lucky win."

From below, a steward was signaling up to the president that all was as ready as it would ever be. The praetor, who was absent-minded, found that he had lost the ceremonial white napkin with which he must signal the start of each race. Camillus pointed out that he was sitting on it. The crowd hushed to an excited buzz as they saw it raised.

Camillus noticed just in time that the trumpeter whose call would be the signal to the hidden slaves who controlled the starting rope was standing only ten paces away, and braced himself. The bronze voice sounded hard and bright through the cool air, and the last notes were drowned by the thunder of hoofs from below that shook the ground like an earthquake. There were eight chariots in the race, two each from the four teams, and they were halfway down the southwest side of the stadium before the dust had settled enough to tell who was in the lead. By the time they had emerged around the far turning post, the position had changed again. Camillus leaned forward, shading his eyes with his hand.

It was a bad-tempered, dangerous race, with two chariots crashing and the charioteer who led the Blues team carried away by hurrying slaves from the bloodstained sand directly below the president's box. His chariot had overturned and thrown him between the hoofs of his nearest rival's horses. Then there were the usual frantic efforts to drag away the crushed wreckage and catch the screaming horses before the remaining six chariots thundered down again out of the straight. But after the last turn the Whites were leading, and to Camillus's intense surprise they came in first and second. Then his spirits lifted, for it was an omen no one could deny. Hylas must be safe. Silently he

pledged an offering to Ceres, patroness of the games, of all
the unlikely deities, if in any way he could bring his mission
to a successful end.

Trumpets sounded again, this time down below the
Palatine Hill. The Emperor had arrived. It was too far for
Camillus to see who was with him. Perhaps the ladies of
the household would not attend today, for it was a long
time since he had been seen in public with the unfortunate
Octavia, his wife. Slowly the morning dragged on, and the
Whites did not win again.

Varro came back late in the morning to find Hylas fast
asleep on his pile of sacks with dried seaweed in his hair.
He was in no mood to let the young man wake up slowly.

Hylas came to with a start to feel a hand on his shoulder,
and he had shot across the storeroom to the back wall
before his eyes were open far enough to recognize his
friend.

"Castor and Pollux, I thought you were the city prefect
at least!" he said, rubbing a skinned elbow. "They've not
hurt Matidia, have they?"

"Matidia? Not her!! A fine time she must have given
them. Here, let me sit down and start from the beginning,
or we shall lose what little sense there is in what's happening. Well, she says after we'd gone it was all quiet for the
rest of the night. The lamp you left can't have shown up
until there was enough daylight to see properly. Then she
said it was as if the furies were loose, the guard turned out
and trotting around the house trying to look as if they
weren't shutting the door when the horse had been gone
for hours. She saw the centurion knock down the porter in

the middle of the peristyle, but they never realized that you'd come over the roofs; lucky you didn't kick any tiles loose."

"Don't," said Hylas, still dizzy even at the memory of the climb.

"For all that, they searched the insula, but she said they didn't seem to know what they were looking for, so she fed them up with a great story of voices in the night that woke her, and two or three moving lights and one of them carried by a Nubian for sure. It took some time."

"But the tribune, didn't he come in in the middle of all this?"

Varro explained. "I was just going when his boy appeared. He must have been asking around the district half the morning. It seems Decianus was suspicious, or that's how I read what the boy could tell me. He may think Camillus is safely out of the way, but I wouldn't put money on the old senator keeping him in the Circus all day. The worst of it is, there's no way of getting to speak to him. What time is it now? Time we both ate something, if you can fancy food in this stink. Then we shall have to wait. He'll go straight home, but he can't be there for hours yet. I daren't leave you here again, so we'll have to go together when the shops open and there are people in the streets."

Varro went through into the front of the shop, and when he came back he had a cucumber and some bread and cheese. While Hylas chewed with a dry mouth, he looked across at his friend. Varro was a very ordinary man, a citizen, but worse off than any slave had been in the household of Caius Pomponius. A man without even a trade, who had to pick up a living where he could between the monthly distributions of grain.

"You said once you'd tell me why you were helping me," Hylas said. "That it wasn't just because you liked saving drowning puppies. You're a lot deeper into something more dangerous than that."

Varro stopped eating, with a hunk of cheese poised on the point of his knife. Then he swallowed the mouthful and grinned. "You don't forget much, do you? Well, yes, like you said, we're both in something dangerous together and that makes it easier to talk. Now you, you're educated, what gods do you believe in? Do you offer your pinch of incense to the divine Emperor, and scramble for the meat when someone in the family decides they want something and they make a sacrifice?"

"I'm not a Roman! No, I'm sorry, I didn't mean to be rude. I know I live in Rome, but I'm Greek-born on both sides and that's how I feel. I always will even if I never have the chance to go there. Everyone has to have something to hang on to, and I'm a Stoic. The philosophers had the highest ideas about life of anyone I've ever heard of. But why did you ask?"

"Well, I thought you'd be the kind of lad who'd at least given it some thought. You don't just live from one day to another. Have you heard of the Way?"

"Which way? Is it one of those eastern religions?"

"Not exactly. Some people call us Christians. I suppose it depends on whether you think a god is someone to get things from, like a greedy child thinks of his father. Our God is one who gives because he wants to, because that's what he's like, and all the children a father gives to are brothers then, aren't they? You have to look out for your brother, and you can't always work out what that's going to cost first. Still, you can trust your father to keep an eye on both of you. Now do you understand?"

It was during the second race after the midday break that Camillus found his chance to escape. All morning he had looked eagerly, but he knew unreasonably, at the sellers of sunflower seeds and nuts who patrolled the walks between the tiers of seats. One of them might be Varro, there might still be a message for him; but none came.

The imperial party in their box to the left had stayed all morning and lunch had been served to them, as it had been to the praetor's party. From some points of view the racing had been good; under the eye of the Emperor the charioteers had taken risks and the accidents had been in proportion. Also the wind had dropped, the early cloud had gone, and the sun now shone from a cloudless sky. The service in the praetor's box had been slow, or perhaps the Emperor was not hungry, for a message came before the last of the food had been cleared away indicating that Nero was growing restive. The praetor, who enjoyed his food, sighed, wiping his mouth on the ceremonial napkin and regretfully putting down a half-gnawed chicken leg.

"Gentlemen, pray continue, but alas the trumpet call of duty summons me," he said.

Camillus took a small dish of pickled sprats back to his seat with him; he had an idea. The first race of the afternoon passed in the pleasant aftermath of a picnic. The praetor leaned back with a wine cup in his hand, Thrasea Paetus ate nuts, Camillus nibbled his fish. Just before the second race started he looked casually behind him. Good, the slaves had cleared away the tables and retired, and some of the party had already left.

This time the main excitement came from the turn at the far end of the course. The first two laps had been uneventful, but as the second gilded egg was lifted from its stand on the high barrier down the middle of the Circus and the chariots started down the straight again, a wave of sound on a different note followed them down the course.

"What is it, what's happening?" mouthed the senator above the din.

Camillus, leaning out, caught the rumor from below. "It's the Blues leader, sir. The crowd can see his offside wheel is working loose. There'll be a smash any moment."

It came at the turn, of course—a pile-up so spectacular that even the senators in their tiers beside the box rose to their feet as one man. The praetor started forward. Camillus popped the largest of the sprats into his mouth, choked realistically into a fold of his toga, and dashed for the doorway.

He was coughing in earnest by the time he got there, for the fish had been very salty, so he was glad to accept the help of an attendant, who beat him on the back and gave him water.

"I think a bone has scratched my throat. Don't disturb him now, but my apologies to the praetor at a convenient time, please. I think I'd better go home and have it attended to."

He did not go out by the main entrance; some instinct took him around by the network of galleries under the stands to an exit opposite the imperial box. It was probably pure fancy, but he could not get away from a feeling of danger. Even down below, the noise was appalling in a muffled way, like a storm at sea heard through the folds of a cloak.

Outside, the streets were almost deserted and he reached his home quickly. It was more than an hour later when the message came that he was waiting for. Hylas and Varro had gone to the back gate, where their unkempt appearance would cause less comment. As he recognized Hylas under the dirt and rags, Camillus could have embraced him out of sheer relief, but the sight of his wife looking down from an upper room stopped him just in time. He took them both to a bench shaded by a loop of vine; only Blandina or Merope could possibly have recognized the slave, but it was as well not to take chances.

"All I could make out from what my boy told me was that you would come here to me, and would I wait for you," he said. "Hylas, have you got it?"

Hylas felt inside the neck of his tunic and drew out the small scroll. "There must be some god I owe a vow to," he said. "I nearly missed it."

Camillus unrolled the paper and smoothed it on his knee; Hylas watched his face go suddenly stiff and blank as he read. Then he looked up sharply.

"You've seen this?"

"Not all, only the first lines to make sure what it was."

Camillus looked down at the paper and then past the two young men, across the courtyard with its small fountain and the statue of a bronze deer grazing at a pool. He held death in his hands as surely as if they cupped a flask of poison. It had already killed the man who had written it; even the knowledge that it existed had been enough.

"This list tells us two things," he said quietly. "First, that

Caius Pomponius was conspiring against the Emperor, and second, that he was killed by someone in the plot with him when he became too dangerous."

Varro looked puzzled. "Why couldn't it have been one of the Emperor's agents who did it, noble Tribune?"

"Because if they had known, everyone on this list would have already been arrested, and I saw several of them in the Circus an hour ago. Hylas, we were right, it could only be Decianus Gallus, or his mother trying to protect him."

"And she was in the house when he wasn't. But she's an old woman."

Camillus interrupted. "I don't know, I don't understand. Was it she who hid this paper in the shrine when she found it in the library, or wherever the senator had left it?"

Hylas felt his heart turn over. He opened his mouth to speak, but Camillus had stood up and turned away. Over his shoulder he said, "I don't know what to do any more. You trusted me, and now I must trust someone else. With my father away I can only go to the next most honest man I know in Rome. We are on the edge of something far too dangerous for me to deal with alone."

"Who?" asked Varro.

"Thrasea Paetus." Camillus shouted to Timon to bring his toga. "He'll be home by now, he usually dines early and alone." He looked up at the sky; it was darkening above the rooftops. "I'll take you down to the kitchen to make sure they look after you, and then we must find a place in the house where Hylas can keep out of the way."

He took two extra slaves to escort him when he left the house. His boy and the torchbearer would not be enough if they stumbled on a brawl while he was carrying the precious scroll; it seemed to burn him as it lay against his chest under his tunic. He remembered that again he had not told Blandina where he was going. Let her wonder; it would give her longer to understand that he was not pleased with her at the moment.

The home of Thrasea Paetus was like its owner, calm and a little bare; Camillus was shown straight into the library. It was almost like visiting a famous physician.

"You are recovered, I hope," said the senator. "It is never wise to underestimate the danger of something stuck in the throat. Still, I'm sorry it shortened what I hope was an enjoyable day for you. Personally I can still not understand the fascination of the Circus, and even less so after this afternoon's accidents."

There was a pause, as he sat back, expecting some routine apology from Camillus for his behavior during the afternoon. But the young tribune sat silent, his hands gripping the arms of his chair and a cold sweat on his forehead, terrified now and with no idea how to start. The senator studied him carefully.

"Camillus, it occurs to me you may be in some difficulty. As you seem to have done me the honor of choosing me as a possible confidant, don't you think you had better tell me what it's about?"

His manner was reassuring. Once Camillus had started, it got easier. The senator was a good listener, he had the gift of physical stillness when his mind was absorbed; even his hands lay motionless before him on the table.

Camillus made his account as brief and businesslike as possible, like a young officer reporting to his commander. Then he handed over the scroll. Thrasea Paetus sat for some time with it in his hands, reading it more than once; then he got up, unlocked a small chest on a table in the corner, put the scroll inside, and relocked it. Camillus just stopped himself from letting out an audible sigh of relief. It was clear that the senator was going to help him.

"If I understand you correctly, you are asking me to do three things: first to believe that a member of one of the oldest families in Rome has been murdered by a close relative, then to help you sort out the evidence you have produced to support your case. Lastly I think you are hoping I shall act on the evidence!"

"I don't know what I was thinking or hoping when I first got mixed up in this yesterday," said Camillus miserably. "I suppose I was just thinking of justice, and I believed Hylas when he told me his story. I still do. But I'm out of my depth now. Even if I could prove who killed Caius Pomponius, I couldn't use the evidence myself. And what about the danger to the Emperor from the other members of the conspiracy?"

"I don't think you need worry about them. After this death we can be sure they will proceed no further. As for your evidence, you were quite right to know that the time had come to hand it over to a superior officer." Thrasea Paetus gave Camillus one of his rare smiles. "Don't belittle your sense of justice either. It was the quality that built everything in Rome which is worth preserving."

"Then you know what we ought to do?" asked Camillus, blushing at the unexpected praise.

"Not yet. Come to me early tomorrow. I must have some time to think, and may Fortuna aid me! I believe we still have a little time, and we could destroy everything by a false move. I don't believe that anyone in the Villa Gallia really suspects you of being more than just a nuisance so far. But, Camillus, keep your escaped slave closely tonight.

He has been missed at last. I remember that Decianus mentioned it this morning when we were on the way to your house. I think the prison governor got tired of waiting for a list and made one of his own. When Decianus checked it, the secretary was missed at once."

"And the steward?"

"Now, that is interesting. Decianus said nothing of him, which may be important."

Camillus remembered for the first time since that morning what Merope had told him. It would be difficult to question her further without arousing his wife's suspicion, but he must try to do it somehow, perhaps early in the morning.

"I will come back at the first hour," he said, "and may the gods bless your deliberations. I won't tell Hylas what you've told me tonight, he must be very short of sleep. Let him rest while he can, he's as safe in my house as anywhere."

XII

HYLAS

HYLAS LAY AWAKE on a pallet on the floor of the small storeroom, where Camillus had arranged that he should sleep for the night. The tribune had come home very late and in a grim mood, and there had been no time to hear anything except that Thrasea Paetus would tell them in the morning what he thought should be done. Varro had gone home then. He had his own concerns to see to and he could not leave Matidia all night without news. In the morning he would come back, and meanwhile what else was there that anyone could do?

Hylas had slept as soon as he lay down, weary after the terrors of the previous night, but now it was after midnight, he was awake again, and his mind was restless. How? How? How? The worst of it was that he could think of no way in which they could add to the facts they had already collected. The house itself would yield up no more secrets; Aulus was dead. Would any of the other slaves have seen or known anything that he did not remember himself? That was the only field that now lay open to them, and no doubt Camillus would go back to the prison in the morning.

He began to think about Domina Faustina, going back to what he had been told of the woman who had married Quintus Pomponius eleven years before Hylas was born. She had been twenty-eight when she had made that second, childless, marriage, and thirty-nine when her husband had died; since then she had ruled the family alone. When Hylas was a small child he had seen her seldom, she had been the awful threat in the upper room who would punish unruly children, and his mother had kept him as far away from her as possible. There had been other children in the house then, and in particular Marcus, who was two years older and content enough to play with him if the slave remembered who he was. There had been the times when they had all gone to the family estate at Nomentum, and those days in the country had been some of the best of his childhood, when instead of playing in two small court-yards, the boys could play across the whole estate and the farms that surrounded it, along the vine terraces and in the hanging branches of the olives. Was it possible that the Domina Faustina he remembered from then, directing the farm workers, could have stabbed her stepson with her own hand? He remembered those strong hands wielding a pruning knife as skillfully as any of the men, and then he thought back to how she had looked on the morning of the Ides when she had come into the master's bedroom.

Yes, she had looked like a dark old queen of the under-world, but her face had been terrible because of what she had known, not what she had seen. It came to him quite certainly now that the horror in her face had not been at some sudden thing. She must have lain awake for hours fearing that some evil thing had been done, with one plan after another racing through her brain. There was only one man alive she would keep her silence for, and that was Decianus.

He found that he, too, was lying stiff and chilled, the hair rising on his neck, as if he had seen the shadow of a murderer with a knife silhouetted at that moment in the uncurtained doorway. What if Decianus had never left the house on the night of the murder? Certainly his litter had gone, but no one except the bearers and the porter knew for certain who had actually been in it, and they were in prison. Matidia had said that Domina Faustina had been walking in the house during the night. She had spoken of no one else, but that might be because they had not asked her. She was old after all, and had mercifully not fully understood all of what was happening. Those questions must be asked her now and he did not see who else could do it.

Hylas did not sleep again. He felt the stubble that now sprouted four days thick on his face; it was a good disguise. He had heard Marcus discussing the operations of the imperial spy network and saying that it was the walk that gave a man away most quickly. He could try to alter that too, with care. Matidia would be awake early and dawn would be the best time, when the streets were crowded with unkempt men and slaves going to their workshops.

Then, just after he heard a cock crow in the last dark hour before the dawn, Hylas knew suddenly that there was someone else in the room with him, a darker shadow just inside the door. His hand slid across the mattress to close around the handle of the knife he had left there, and the blade must have glinted in what little light there was, because a sound came from the crouching shadow, some thing between a gasp and a squeak.

"No, Hylas, it's me."

Hylas raised himself on his elbows. "Merope?"

She dropped down on the edge of the mattress, pulling her dark cloak around her in the night chill. "I thought I'd got the wrong storeroom, you were lying so quietly."

"How did you know I was here?"

"I saw you yesterday. Don't worry, I don't think anyone else would have recognized you, but I knew you weren't in prison, so I was on the lookout. You're planning something, aren't you, with my new master? I saw it in his face when I asked him about you."

"Merope, what are you doing here at this time of the morning? Someone could have seen you coming in to me." Hylas found that he was not pleased to see the girl, even though he had missed her confident chatter after she had left his master's house as a wedding present to Blandina. All he could think about now was Matidia, and the questions he must ask her.

"Don't worry, they wake late here, Domina Faustina would be horrified! But, Hylas, I've got to tell someone and the master never seems to have time. I've tried to speak to him and he's always in a hurry. It wasn't Aulus killed Caius Pomponius, was it? Do you think it was Assinius?"

Hylas sat up and pulled the blanket round his shoulders, for he was shivering with more than the cold air. He had thought that there was no one but Matidia who could help them now; how had he forgotten Merope? She had been at the villa on the day before the murder and her sharp eyes missed nothing.

"I'm sorry," he said, "you scared me, creeping in like that, I'd been thinking horrors all night. You're right, it wasn't poor Aulus, but I don't see how it could have been Assinius either. What were you trying to tell Camillus?"

"Two things really. First, Assinius, he's been up to something for a long time, nasty creepy soft-sandaled man. Three days after the wedding, when my mistress went to visit Domina Livonia for the first time, I saw him at the villa of the Galli, talking to Decianus. They didn't notice me, they seemed too worried, but Assinius had no business to be there. Whatever plotting it is that's been going on, Assinius is deep in it, and I think he had warning to get away from the house before the murder was discovered, and Decianus is hiding him. I saw him again when we were leaving the villa on the evening of the funeral and I told Camillus, but I think he had something else on his mind and he didn't seem to take in what it meant."

"What do you think it did?"

"I don't know, you know far more about what's happened than I do, but could it have been Assinius who let the murderer into the house?"

"Or did it himself? No, Merope, it can't be quite as simple as that, but it fits with the rest of the pattern; at least I'm sure it must if I could just see where." He sat with his arms clasped around his knees, thinking hard while Merope waited quietly beside him. Camillus would curse himself when he knew the information that had been waiting all the time under his own roof.

Then Hylas raised his head again. "You said you had two things to tell."

Merope made a worried sound. "I'm glad I can tell this to you, not him. It's Blandina, I don't know what she's done, but it's something she's ashamed of. She didn't cry like that just for her father, she was frightened, and it was a good way of stalling for time while she saw what would happen. Now she's happy again; whatever it was she feared doesn't appear to be happening, so she's stopped pinching me and hurting the monkey."

"The monkey?"

"Yes, poor Scipio, she knocked him right across the

room on the morning when they brought the news about her father."

"Oh, Merope! So that was it." Hylas saw again a tiny sharp picture of everything that had happened in the peristyle when he had come back to the villa with Camillus on the afternoon before the murder. So it had been the monkey who had escaped and found the scroll, and Blandina had not been able to get it back into the library. It had all come from that, and from Blandina's blind terror when she saw what she had in her hands. She had lacked the courage to go to her father, and it had cost him his life. No wonder she had cried.

"No, I can't explain it all now," he said aloud. "Someone must tell Camillus. I'll do it later, I've got to go out on an errand of my own soon. Fortune bless you, Merope, and don't worry any more. Go quickly before anyone else wakes up."

He got up a little later, when he heard the first stirrings outside in the courtyard. Color was barely showing in the eastern sky above the roofs when the porter let him out. He would be back almost before Camillus was awake. Perhaps he was being foolish, but the tribune himself could hardly go back to the insula now that it had been searched, and it might be hours before Varro came. He left a message with the sleepy porter, and began to thread his way through the web of alleys behind the narrow main thoroughfares of the city.

The guard was still there outside the gate of the Villa Pomponia. That surprised him, because with the master buried and the slaves in prison, what could the authorities fear except the burglary of an empty house? And that was the responsibility of the heirs. It would have been mad to pass the gate itself, but he could not resist crossing the street higher up so that he could glance quickly down. It told him nothing. The feeling of adventure that had come from making plans, safe inside the walls of the tribune's house, was fading fast. He found it was difficult to keep up the limp he had tried to assume. After several wrong turns he managed to find the narrow and smelly back entrance to the flats; already the daytime racket had started, and he attracted no attention as he climbed quickly up the stairs past children coming down to empty slops. Those men who worked seemed already to have left.

He paused just below Matidia's room. There was no one in sight. He used the knock Varro had shown him and heard the old woman stir and grunt inside and the bolt shift back.

Hylas was inside the room before Matidia had time to see it was not Varro. When she did, she hugged him as if he were really kin, and began to putter determinedly about, trying to find something to eat.

"Leave that now, Auntie, there isn't time. We've got to talk," he said. "I must be back at the tribune's house within the hour."

"He's a very nice young man, a good friend for the young master."

"Yes, Auntie, but it wasn't him I came to talk about. Are you in a remembering mood? Can you remember what you told us that first morning about how you sat on the balcony all night, so you knew who was wakeful in the house?"

The old face creased into a pattern of knowing wrinkles. "Did I tell you that? Well, it was true; when the children were small and sick in the night I often knew of it before their grandmother, that's for sure. She didn't pace about as much in those days. It's been worse the last months. Almost like the poor daft girl in the room below whose baby died and who would get up to look for it."

"You mean it was as if the lady was looking for something?" Hylas's heart was in his mouth. Time was short, but he must not hurry the old woman.

"Nothing she ever found that I saw. No, it was more restlessness. Let me think now, that last night; did I say the moon was low? Only three days ago. Now by Venus, who favors dark nights, it seems longer than that, but she had a lamp, I remember."

Hylas grinned. "Who, Venus?"

She laughed appreciatively. "Venus needs no lamp to go about her business. I remember the glow of it, as if she was shading it with her hand, and the color of her blue cloak just showing. And it went here and there, and through to the front and stayed there, and I was almost dozing off when it came back fast, and not as shielded, and the light went down the far side and behind the pillars and out of sight."

The old woman stopped suddenly while Hylas held his breath. "Try and see it again, Auntie," he said quietly, careful not to break her mood. "Think it's a picture in front of you. When Madam came back did you see the blue cloak again?"

Her eyes looked wide and unfocused. It's not going to work, he thought. Then suddenly she was very much alive and back with him.

"No, by the dog, I didn't. She was wearing something dark and brownish and the feet didn't sound the same. But I saw her gray hair."

"Other people have gray hair." But not Decianus, he thought, he's still dark.

"Was it the murderer and did I see him?" She put up a hand and fumbled at her trembling mouth. "Oh, lad, did I see him, and Madam there too, and me not knowing what was going on?"

He tried to get hold of the restless, fumbling old hands to comfort her. "I don't know what you saw, Auntie, that's for wiser heads than ours to work out. But someone was there, and that's enough to mean life to my mother and the others. Don't you worry about Madam, think of the lives you've saved with your good memory. Now I've got to go and tell the tribune all about it. If Varro comes, let him know I've been here and what you said."

"They say there's plague in the Subura quarter," she said inconsequentially, as he released her and started toward the door.

"Good thing you're safe up here; don't go gadding that way yourself," he said, with a laugh.

"Nor you, neither! Now hold still, who knows what streets you'll be off down, wait while I make you one of my posies."

He stood impatiently while she sorted through her bunches and jars of herbs, but in kindness he could not go before she had finished. She collected her finds into a bunch and found a small cloth bag with a string at the neck to hold them. "There, my dear, rue and vervain and rosemary and some of my secrets you wouldn't know the names of. That'll keep you safe, you being a good-living lad and likely to keep away from bad company."

Much opportunity I have, he thought, as he slipped away down the back stairs. That was clearly part of the patter she gave all her clients. He had the small pouch in the front of his tunic, slightly prickly but smelling strong and clean.

In the archway at the bottom he stopped, back out of sight from the alley that was hardly broader than his own shoulders. Even here it was bright daylight, and the way back to the tribune's house seemed suddenly long and exposed. Camillus would tell him he had been mad to try it alone in the morning and he would be right. But it might be that what he had learned from Matidia had been worth the risk, even though he could still not be sure that Decianus had been in the villa during the night. Yet someone had opened the door to the gray-haired man in the brown cloak, and he must have been the one who used the knife. None of it was going to be easy to prove, but after his talk with Merope it was all clear now. Bluff was perhaps the only possible weapon. Thrasea Paetus would see that.

It would be difficult now to get back with this vital information through the bright streets. If he had something to carry, a load like the ones porters carried on their heads, that might give him both a reason to be out and a disguise. Under the last twist of the stairs he found a rotting sack half full of straw. Perhaps it was someone's discarded bedding; if so, his nose told him the reason it had been thrown away. He must put up with that, he did not smell too sweet himself. With the sack balanced on his head the streets seemed possible.

He knew very soon that the idea had been a bad one. The sack was too rotten to hold together; the more he tried to keep it steady, the more his fingers went through the sodden straw. Handfuls began to fall out as he tottered along, then one end sagged and tore away, coming down over his eyes so that he bumped into a swag of pots hanging outside a bronzesmith's, making them chime like a festival. The owner shouted after him as he broke into a trot, trying now to find somewhere to leave his stinking load. But here the streets were wider and more crowded; he tried to find a quieter turning and was lost almost at once.

Hylas knew he was not being rational now; his heart was thumping and he could feel the blood hot in his face as he pounded uphill, trying to keep his eyes clear. The lay of the road seemed to be steering him into a series of left-hand turns. When the sack at last fell into two halves, the contents landing around his feet so that he looked like a donkey foddered down in a stall, he was in a broader place, but where he could not see as he coughed and rubbed the dust out of his eyes.

What he first saw was the polished breastplate of a centurion of the city guard. Then his eyes traveled down and saw that the moldy straw had spilled on the officer's heavy laced sandals, and some wisps had caught in the folds of his split leather skirt. Very deliberately he brushed them away and stepped back, and Hylas saw his chest swell. He was about to receive from very close range what the officer's century usually suffered on the parade ground when he was displeased. The shout never came.

Instead, Hylas found his hands seized and inspected. In the strong April sunlight he could see himself that even under the dirt they did not look like a porter's hands; besides, he could never quite get the ink out of the roughened skin on his first finger.

"Carpus!" the man bellowed over his shoulder. "It was a secretary we wanted, wasn't it? Look what I've found!"

Hylas gazed past him and in the same direction. The

door that had opened to him so often with the promise of security was just across the street, the door of the Villa Pomponia, with the guard outside it staring at him in amusement. He had walked in a circle.

The mind doesn't take in things all at once, he thought to himself, as the cords bit into his wrists and he was jerked almost off his feet. A woman might be able to faint, to get away out of herself for a moment; fainting makes people sympathetic. Who pities a captured runaway slave? Only another slave. The guard was dragging his arms forward at an impossible angle, delighted with his prize and hurrying to hand him over; it made it hard to breathe and he could not see where he was putting his feet. What did that matter? There was going to be pain now, and nothing more before he died but fear, getting worse and darker, and himself changing into a screaming, cringing thing, something not human. He had thought he was a Stoic, but what did Zeno teach about being tortured to death? They would have to do that, wouldn't they? He had escaped and now someone had remembered him and the hunt had started. It would not be Aulus now who was the scapegoat, but a younger, more long-lasting victim. And Camillus would not know, not in time before the pain started, and even after, could he stop it? How long did it take?

The guard halted at a crossing where an expensive litter was passing surrounded by a large escort of slaves. Hylas bent double and was sick, but not as sick as he would have liked to be, for he had refused Matidia's breakfast. When they moved on again, he nearly did faint. The guard turned around to him.

"Oh, we're going to have some sport with you!"

That helped. Fury seemed to clear Hylas's head. His

chin went up and he began to think hard, throwing his mind back, out of all this horror, to the heroes of literature and history who had been tormented and had borne it nobly. Who was the Roman general who had gone back to be tortured to death by the Carthaginians in fulfillment of a vow? Was it Regulus? The only thought that he could keep in his mind now was that Camillus might never know about the man in brown and it would all have been for nothing.

The gates of the prison that had been opened for Camillus two days before closed on Hylas with a very different clang. He was almost oblivious of his surroundings by now. He had never seen Macrobius, so he did not know that he was not there, or wonder why he was being taken at once down the steps to the lower gallery without questioning, while the guard clattered off to find the governor. Camillus would have noticed at once that there was a difference in the cages of prisoners, that the guards were standing well back with rags bound around their faces and that the smell was different.

Hylas saw none of this. He was kicked the last four steps and landed in a heap in the filth that ran in runnels on the concrete floor. Not many of the prisoners came forward at the noise to stare at the grating except those in the cell at the end. Hylas heard his name, but did not look up, even when he landed on his knees inside, not until hands were tearing at the knots that fastened the cords around his bleeding wrists. Then his mother put her arms around him while he still knelt there, and cried.

XIII

FORTUNA OF THE TRIPLE GARLAND

CAMILLUS WAS STANDING in the courtyard of his father's house, too shaken to move or speak at once. Varro, small, bandy-legged, and scruffy, had been crying so much that Camillus had not understood at once what he was trying to tell him. So Hylas had almost certainly gone to his death because he had not known that the hunt was up, and that was because Camillus had had a stupid idea that the slave would get a better night's sleep for not knowing. And now this. Anyone but a fool would have known it was a possibility, anyone but a fool would have found time to listen to Merope. She had recognized Varro at once from the upper balcony and come down to hear the news and tell them both what she had told Hylas four hours before. There had been no time for Merope to cry, for she had to keep an innocent and untroubled face before her mistress, whatever despair was in her heart.

Camillus looked quickly at the sun above the roofs. It was midmorning, and Varro had seen Hylas taken by the guards at the first hour after dawn.

"I still don't understand why," he said. "Varro, what made him go to Matidia's room in the first place?"

"It was to ask her about the night of the murder, what

she saw. Auntie is certain now that there was someone else in the house, a man in brown, but she was crying a lot and she couldn't tell me what Hylas was really thinking about."

Camillus shouted for the boy to bring his toga. "I've got to go to the prison at once. I can think of some excuse when I get there, Macrobius isn't clever. Hylas is the only one who can explain, and with him in there, our time has run out. Varro, you left Matidia to come to me. I don't want to let you go, but should you be back with her?"

Varro's weeping had reached the sniffling stage. He made a snort that was almost a laugh. "No, I can stay here. There's a baby being born across the landing from her room and Auntie will have plenty to take her mind off Hylas. Besides, she doesn't understand properly what it means to Hylas, being in prison, and I wouldn't be able to keep it from her long. She's better occupied with something else."

Camillus walked quickly through the crowded streets. Festival or no festival, most of the shops were open again. The holiday just meant that there were more people to stroll and peer and slow him down. With his mind racing he did not see who it was who had taken him by the shoulder until he had jerked back so violently that he might have been a prisoner on the run himself.

"Steady! Who am I supposed to be, the chief of police?" asked Galerius mildly. "Where are you off to so fast? We thought you must have left Rome till I spotted you in the president's box at the Circus yesterday."

"Let me go, Galerius, I can't stop now. I'll try and see you tomorrow, honestly I will." Then his mind pulled itself far enough loose from its distress to see the puzzled concern on his friend's face.

"Bad trouble?" asked Galerius quietly. "Caius Pomponius?"

"Yes, partly. And I will see you tomorrow. It must be over one way or the other by then."

"And I can't help?"

"Only by letting me go now."

Galerius put both hands on his shoulders and gave him a shake that was part affection and part exasperation, then he was lost in the crowd. Camillus went on more slowly. There had not even been time to send a message to Thrasea Paetus, so he did not know what the senator would have decided before he knew of this new disaster. But that must wait. It seemed that he himself was always rushing here and there and doing things in the wrong order. He ought to think what he was going to say before he reached the prison; he would not be expected to know either of the existence of Hylas or that he had been captured. It would be fortunate if Macrobius was in the same compliant mood as last time.

His face was very bleak as he paused under the portico of a small temple wreathed for the festival. A small woman, wizened as a withered grape, sat bunched on the top step. Old women had brought luck to the beginning of this whole horrible business, or at least one had.

"Whose temple is this, mother?" he asked.

She gave him the look of one who has probably never crossed the city in her life to a stranger who is ignorant of her own small warren. "Our Fortuna of the triple garland, of course!"

Fortuna again. Last night Thrasea Paetus had invoked her, and now it seemed an omen that he had paused here. He vowed a silver statue to the goddess if he found Hylas able to tell him what he needed to know. He would have offered gold for the chance that he was still untouched, but some miracles are unreasonable and asking for them would only offend any sensible god.

Macrobius did not seem surprised to see him, but he was not very affable. Camillus knew a frightened man when he saw one and wondered what had happened, but some time had to be spent first on the usual courtesies.

"So even during the festival they keep you here, and a sunless place I must confess I find your prison, however reliable in other ways," he said.

"Sunless!" said Macrobius moodily. "Downright unhealthy, it's too near the river. But you can't complain the moment you're appointed, and after that I suppose you get used to it. Then what ought to be expected happens, and by Castor and Pollux we've a bad dose of it now."

"Dose of what?"

"How do I like to see my prisoners leave? Freed or punished, not carted out feet first, untried. It's plague, sir, I'm sorry to say. I should have told you at once, you might not have liked to come even this far. Decianus Gallus was here earlier, but he wouldn't stay to hear the interrogation of the new lad brought in this morning, not when I'd told him. It wouldn't have been so bad, only my idiot sergeant put him straight down with the others for an hour, and there were three deaths there yesterday and two today already. How can I ever get anything done or keep clear returns for the prefect when I can't even get down to my own prisoners?"

"Decianus Gallus was here? I had hoped to save him that trouble. And you say that he did not speak to the newly captured slave? Perhaps I could still see him."

"Well, sir, I've got my guards down there, of course. But as for you, sir . . . and I daren't bring him back up again."

"Then, Macrobius, I will go down. I think my constitution is sufficiently healthy to resist the humors of the plague for a short time. Strange that the slave has only just been traced. A secretary, wasn't he?"

"As I said to the noble Decianus Gallus," complained the man, "I can't be expected to know the members of his mother's household as well as he does. A certain number I was given and wrote down. If one was missing off the list he sent, I couldn't know until then, could I? But he wasn't satisfied. I only hope we get something worth the trouble from this one; that would cover a lot."

"He's been questioned, then?"

"We made a start. But then they brought up the two bodies from this morning and that put the lads off getting as close as they needed to the prisoner, even though he's only been in the cells an hour. You're sure you want to go down, sir?"

"I know my way, Macrobius, I won't be long."

The man was sweating. Everyone had some secret horror, and it might be another of the workings of Fortuna that plague seemed to be Macrobius's weak spot. Camillus followed the guard down the oozing stairs to the lower levels for the second time.

Hylas was sitting on the floor near the front of the cell. Camillus stood back, looking at him through the grille. The slave had not seen him, and for one wild moment he seemed almost unharmed. Then Camillus noticed the way he was sitting. Nissa was in front of him, braced with her arms around her knees; Hylas, curled on his right side and staring at the ground, was leaning most of his weight on her.

The guard, his face wrapped in a cloth soaked in vinegar, unlocked the gate and Camillus went in. He could not be bothered with what the man thought of a military tribune who went down on his knees in front of a tortured slave.

Hylas looked up when the key rattled, a small, careful movement of his head alone. It was not a day since they had seen each other, but now Hylas's skin seemed stretched over bones grown already sharp; his hair was stuck to his forehead with sweat and a bruise was darkening across his left cheek.

"Hylas, what did they do?" Camillus asked quietly, laying a hand very gently on the young man's left arm, which lay motionless in his lap.

Hylas flinched and his voice sounded clumsy because his lips were swollen. "I fell down the steps and sprained my wrist. It would have been all right, only they tied me up and it . . . it had to take my weight."

Camillus could see the blood on his tattered tunic now, and how it had been put back on loosely, not girdled over what lay beneath.

"You were flogged?"

"Yes." There was a long pause, then: "I was lucky, I think, it was all they had time for. The sergeant didn't seem to know what was wanted from me, so it was routine till Decianus came. And then he was frightened and didn't stay, so they untied me and brought me back here."

His voice was flat with the effort of holding it steady while the pain still battered at him as if the lash were falling. "I've never been flogged before," he said, looking down again and not at Camillus's face. "Caius didn't mark valuable slaves. I'm glad I was valuable before."

"Hylas, what did Matidia tell you? What made you go to her?"

The slave did not answer at once. Camillus, watching him, understood something of how bad pain makes it difficult to get thoughts clear. He shifted restlessly; the rough concrete of the floor was already bruising his knees even through the thick folds of his toga.

Hylas looked up and the corners of his mouth twitched. "I'm sorry, I'll try to be quick." He breathed once, deeply but carefully. "You see, I was thinking in the night, and I don't know why unless a god told me, but I was sure that the mistress didn't kill the master. I remembered Matidia talking about seeing her moving about the house, but we never really asked her exactly what it was she saw. She did see the mistress first, but then it was someone else, a man with gray hair and a brown cloak who went toward the master's room. Matidia couldn't hear if Domina Faustina spoke to him, or if the house doors were opened, not from that height, but it gave me a clue. And now I'm here I've put it all together."

His head dropped forward again. Nissa twisted around and tried to arrange him more comfortably.

"The porter knew what had happened, noble Tribune. I got the story from him after they'd taken Hylas upstairs," she said. "He's not clever and he was very frightened and he hadn't understood what it meant. Decianus Gallus never left the house. It was Assinius who went away in the litter. The porter thought nothing of it at the time; there seemed no reason why a stepbrother should not spend a night in the house. He must have waited in one of the guest rooms off the atrium until the house was quiet. He would know that things wouldn't be done properly with the steward away, and he was unlikely to be found."

"But did his mother know he was there?"

"I don't think so. I was with her and she went straight to bed. The porter doesn't remember much more; he went to sleep and didn't wake till morning, and then he had a bad head. He thought his beer tasted strange at the time. Assinius must have drugged it."

"But Decianus didn't wear a brown cloak and his hair is dark. What was he doing?"

Hylas said in his tired voice, "He was waiting to let the murderer in. He had sent Assinius with a message to someone else, some other name on the list. He wouldn't use the knife himself, he hasn't his mother's nerve, and murderers aren't hard to come by in Rome. He waited until the porter was asleep, and the man scratched on the door and he let him in. Only the mistress came down and saw something. When it was over, she must have locked the gates behind the two of them. It was all she could do; he was her son, and she might not have known exactly what had been done. I know it must have happened like that, my lord, even though I don't suppose we can ever prove it." He paused, then went on even more quietly. "In spite of everything I'm glad we tried."

Camillus looked down at him helplessly, while the full horror of what it meant to be a slave and in prison sank deep into his mind. There could be no respite for Hylas now from the cold and stinking darkness of this cell. What he needed was a clean, quiet bed, and Nissa to wash his back and feed him when he had rested. Here there was little she could do except be there, and no other comfort, ever, unless he himself could free the household of Pomponius.

As Camillus saw Hylas lying quietly in the dirt at his feet, he felt something that had come to him only a few times so far in his life, and that he could never have dreamed he would feel for a slave. It was that nothing and no one in Rome or the whole Empire beyond was so important, so infinitely valuable as this boy not very much younger than he was, who had come to him as a suppliant and was now his friend as even Galerius and Marcus had never been. There was only one way he could show what he felt, one gift that Hylas in his suffering could understand and accept, the gift of his own hope even though he must quarry it out of a heart in which there was only bleakness and despair.

He bent close. There seemed nowhere he could touch Hylas without hurting him. Then Camillus laid both hands on his knee, and the cold, dirty fingers moved to touch them.

"The proof must be there. Thrasea Paetus will get it even if I have to hold Decianus while we break every bone in his body. And I've talked to Merope at last, she's told me everything she told you, so I know the whole story now." He paused, but there was nothing for it, Hylas deserved the full truth. "Even about Blandina, she told me that too. I don't know how Nissa could have guessed my wife had something to hide. I suppose it was because she knows her so much better than I do. And now pray, Hylas my friend, to whatever gods you believe in, offer them what you like, we'll pay your vows together on a happier day. I will not waste an hour now, knowing that each hour here means a month to you. Rest and think what you will do when you are free."

Hylas's eyes had been shut. At that they opened, sunken, but hopeful beyond possibility. "Free?"

"As the gods are my witness, free of this place and free of the family of Pomponius."

XIV

DOMINA FAUSTINA

CAMILLUS FINISHED his story. It was already late morning as he sat back, slumped miserably in his chair in the bare, sunny library; the leaves of a climbing rose had spread across a high window, and they were making a dancing pattern of shadow that shifted slowly across the floor toward his feet. Then the senator stood up suddenly and put both hands down flat on the writing table.

"Attack! That, as the divine Caesar must have said, is the defense both of the cornered rat and the hard-pressed general!"

"You mean that what we can't find out any other way, we have to ask?"

"Certainly. That part of the story which your brave young slave has discovered should be enough to bait a trap. Camillus Rufus, last night I had decided to give you what help I could for no other reason than justice. Now I can see that if Hylas were the only slave to be saved, he would be worth the trouble."

Camillus stood up too. "Do you mean, Senator, that we simply go to Decianus and ask him what happened?" He supposed he had known for hours that this was what was coming, but he still felt sick at the thought. "Isn't that asking him to condemn himself?"

"I think he will be able to shift the guilt from his own

shoulders, but for us to discover the truth it must seem for a while to hang above him. But then, as I said, attack! All we need is an alternative murderer, and your man in brown should not be impossible to trace even in the warrens of Rome. Then, if the name of a former consul still carries any weight, I should be able to organize the inquiry so that the slaves get a fair hearing. That should be enough."

"And you want me to come with you?" For one wild moment Camillus wondered if he could avoid the coming ordeal. How would he ever be able to face Blandina again if he had been present when these things were said and done? Then he wondered if he wanted to.

Briefly the impassive hawk eyes softened. "I very much regret it, but you too must go through your hour of trial. This case was begun by you, and it may yet be that some word of yours, not mine, will tip the balance. Now we must wait an hour until we can be sure that Decianus is at home, and then may Fortuna go with us!"

They were kept standing for what seemed a long time in the atrium of the villa of the Galli, before Decianus came through from the family rooms behind. He looked at them coldly, the affability of the day before quite gone.

"I understand that you have asked to speak with my mother, Thrasea Paetus?"

"With you both."

"You must be aware that she is still in great grief at our loss. Can you not state your business to me alone?"

Camillus, watching him closely, saw a pulse beating in his forehead. He was frightened. He knew something was up, or he would not have spoken so coldly to an important man.

"The matter is personal to you both, and so urgent that

any delay could cause great harm to your whole family. I crave your noble mother's indulgence," said Thrasea Paetus. "I will ask her again." He called irritably to a slave as he went through the archway that led to the women's rooms. The small hall to which they were taken was on the dark side of the peristyle. From the faded paint on the walls and the air of somewhere that has been furnished hastily with what can be spared from other rooms, it seemed that Livonia had been forced to prepare a private sitting room for her formidable mother-in-law. Although it was early in the afternoon, a lamp had already been lit beside the high-backed chair in the center, almost as if it were the shrine of a god. Then Domina Faustina entered, dressed in black; she crossed the room without looking at them and settled herself with her hands on her knees in her pool of lamp-light. Now she did look like one of the small terra-cotta statues of goddesses that were sold everywhere, solid and a little misshapen. Camillus wished that he could leave his offering and go; then his mind jerked back to Hylas.

"Senator, you have some pressing reason for what you must realize is an intrusion?" she asked, ignoring Camillus.

"Noble lady, as a magistrate of this city I have certain duties to perform that can be onerous and distasteful, but in the cause of justice they must be endured. Decianus Gallus, are we free in this room to speak frankly?"

Decianus understood. He nodded to the steward who had been hovering in the half-open doorway; the man went out and closed the door behind him.

"I have come at this untimely hour because there are points that must be settled before the inquiry into the death of the late Caius Pomponius can begin," the senator continued.

"You have authority for your inquiries? We have asked for none to be made," said Domina Faustina.

"The authority I have will soon become very clear," said the senator with a coolness that almost made Camillus gasp out loud. "Four days ago your stepson was murdered at a time when your home was locked for the night, and you were alone with him and with your household slaves. Domina Faustina, I must ask you to remember again what happened early the next morning when the body was discovered, so that we can be quite sure of the facts of the case. You were still in your room then?"

"I am no longer a young woman to rise before dawn! Yes, I was still in my room when a girl came in with some incoherent story of tragedy. I put on my cloak and went to see what was the matter. I expected to find that perhaps a valuable vase had been broken in the morning cleaning; what I found was a slave with his hands dripping with blood and my son lying cruelly stabbed with his own knife in his own bed."

"And so you assumed that it was the slave, Aulus, who had killed him?"

"What else was I to think when the man stood there before me with his master's blood upon him? Surely the phrase 'red-handed' fits such a case?"

"And yet I understand that by the time you came down from your room Aulus had already washed the blood from his hands in the fish tank in the atrium, and the body was already cold and stiff. Can it, then, be possible that the blood on the slave came from the act of murder itself, which must have happened hours before? If Aulus had killed his master during the night, he would not have waited so long before trying to escape, and he would certainly not have touched him when he went back at dawn. He can only have expected to find his master alive. Did you see the wound yourself, Domina Faustina?"

Her hands curled and clenched upon her knees. "I did not."

"But you saw the hilt of the knife that made it?"

"It belonged to the toilet set laid out in my son's room. It had an ivory handle."

"The knife Aulus used to pare his master's nails. It does not seem likely that he would have used a weapon that pointed so directly to himself if he had in fact committed the crime. Perhaps your son's valet may already have suffered unjustly."

Decianus twitched restlessly. "That had certainly not been decided when the wretched man died. But who could it have been except the slaves, when the house had been locked for the night?"

"Could not some murderer have entered from outside?"

"As my son says, that would have been impossible with the doors fastened from within."

"And does the evidence of your steward bear this out?"

"Assinius? Of course. Has he not been questioned with the others?" asked Domina Faustina.

She doesn't know he's missing, thought Camillus. That's something else she hasn't been told. And as he watched her, his hands within the concealing folds of his toga clenched so that the nails bit into the palms, he felt the first twinge of pity for the stiff little figure before him. For a moment he would almost have stopped Thrasea Paetus if he could, but then he remembered Hylas, and the slow dripping of the hours in the prison beside the river.

"Noble lady, your steward was not in the house when

the guard came. He has not been seen since the night before the murder. You were correct when you asked in vain as you saw the body, 'Is there no man left alive here?' "

"How did you know that? Who told you what was said?" Decianus took a step forward. "The steward must have slipped away in the confusion of the early morning. He could have had business in the market."

"There are witnesses who will say he did not. Indeed, Decianus Gallus, I think both you and the examining magistrate will be surprised by the number of witnesses!"

Decianus made an attempt at a laugh. "Really, Senator, you are making it seem as if we in this room are on trial, not just helping you to establish some of the facts; and why we should do it before Camillus Rufus you have yet to explain."

Thrasea Paetus let the silence lengthen on, long heartbeats past what Camillus thought he could bear. He saw Domina Faustina's hands twist and clench on her lap again and the color ebb slowly from Decianus's face. Then the senator turned and sat down in the chair that had been put ready for him, settled his toga, and took out a small scroll from the folds across his breast. He looked across at them as steadily as he had so often done at those who had been brought to him for judgment in the courts of Rome.

"Decianus Gallus, I think you will indeed find that this is a court, and one where you are likely to receive a fairer hearing than would those slaves we have already spoken of. Camillus, will you now tell us what you told me and what I wrote down this morning: your account of the last hours of Caius Pomponius Afer. Yes, Decianus, what you are about to hear has already been written down and left in safe keeping."

Camillus heard his own voice speaking, almost before he had thought what he was going to say, stammering on the first sentence and then gaining conviction.

"On the afternoon before the Ides the whole family were together at the Villa Pomponia. I left with my wife, but you remained behind and had dinner with my father-in-law and Domina Faustina. Toward the end of the meal you quarreled with Caius Pomponius. You accused him of great indiscretion in a matter that you had on hand. He had committed names to writing in a way that could endanger you."

The right hand of Thrasea Paetus closed around the scroll he was holding. Decianus was staring at it in sick fascination.

"After your mother had left the room, you made as if to go home. Assinius the steward went with you to the front gate; he had already found time to drug the porter's beer. It was he, sent on an errand of your own, who left in the curtained litter. You remained behind in the guest room near the family shrine in the atrium. It was almost midnight when you heard the scratching at the door that you were waiting for, and you opened it quietly with the keys from the porter's belt, to a man you were expecting.

"He knew what he had come to do, but in that moment you were horrified to find your mother, unable to sleep, walking in the peristyle in her blue cloak."

Domina Faustina was lying back in her chair with her eyes closed; she opened her mouth as if she was about to speak, but no words came. Camillus knew that now was the moment when the last and most wounding blow must be struck. He was quite absorbed, all memories of former schoolboy debates forgotten, unaware that his youth and sternness were far more telling than the authority of Thrasea Paetus could ever have been. As he watched him, the senator knew that not the least of the chances he had taken that afternoon had been successful.

"You did not tell your mother that the murderer of her stepson was already inside the house, but you persuaded her to return to her room. She was distressed at your unexpected presence, fearful of what it meant, but she went. So she did not hear the footsteps of the man in a brown cloak with gray hair as he crossed the peristyle, or the rhythm of the fountain change as he came out of the room next to the library a little later and washed his hands beneath it. When the man had gone, you went to her again and she came down with you to let you out, no doubt hoping that you had been making your peace with your stepbrother; she locked the gate behind you and replaced the keys. Her horror must have been all the greater when a slave's voice woke her with the news of disaster on the morning of the Ides of April."

"No!" The old woman had come bolt upright, with her eyes wide open, and in her face the cold passion of a Medusa. "My son Decianus left the house in his own litter, and slept the night in his bed. It is true that I was walking that night in my house, because I could not sleep. In their quarrel my sons had let slip the few words that I needed to confirm my worst fears. For months I had been watching Caius with increasing dread, for it seemed to me that he was behaving like a mad child who throws stones at a sleeping lion. Thrasea Paetus, only you in this room can clearly remember the days of the Emperor Gaius Caligula, for it is twenty years since he was murdered. I think when

one has once lived in a house that has been struck by
lightning, it is reasonable to fear thunderstorms. And I
have seen such a storm gathering above Rome from the
very hour that the Divine Claudius died. Caius was right to
honor him, but not when doing so made him forget what
life under Caligula was like and how it may still be under
Nero."

Camillus thought back to what he had been told about
the Emperor who had died before he was born. It had been
a time of excitement and spectacle, of political chaos fer-
mented by a capricious, half-mad boy. He realized that
Domina Faustina was watching him.

"Yes, you, Camillus Rufus, may be thinking that it was
exciting to live then. I remember only the honest and noble
men, citizens and senators, who had spent their lives in the
service of Rome, screamed at and insulted, humiliated in
public and dragged away to death, with even the dignity of
suicide denied them. I saw what was done to their families.
Caius was a young man, safe with his legions, safer before
the enemy spears than we were in our own city. He knew
nothing of how we lived then, he did not realize that Nero
may become as dangerous as Caligula. He could laugh at
the danger the least glance of Nero could bring, and drink
a toast to Octavia in memory of the better days under her
father, Claudius. He was fool enough even to plot, and to
write down names, which could have brought death not
only to himself but to his whole family, and the confisca-
tion of what we had been able to keep together even during
the worst times. Both my sons were guilty, but he most of
all; when I knew there was no other way I killed him with
my own hands. He was not of my body like Decianus."

"Madam, you killed him? You went into your son's bedroom that night, took a knife, and killed him as he slept?" Thrasea Paetus had also risen from his seat and Camillus saw the scroll crushed in his right hand.

"Who better knew where the knife would be? Are you doubting my strength, Senator, or my fixity of purpose? I think no member of my household has ever had reason to doubt that. And as to the knowledge of where to strike, as I have reminded you, I lived under Caligula, when one acquired many strange skills. I am not unfamiliar with the knives used in my vineyards; the wise steward learns the skills of his servants."

Out of the corner of his eyes Camillus saw a movement, but his whole attention was still fixed upon Domina Faustina. Had they been wrong after all, had Matidia made a mistake and was the murderer really this unlikely old woman with her face of stone who stood before them? And if they had been so wrong, what could they do now? Even Thrasea Paetus was silent.

Domina Faustina sat down with the stiff care of the very old. The color that had come into her face as she spoke faded, leaving it as gray and heavy as before. Then something seemed to move behind her eyes, a great flash of emotion vivid as forked lightning, which lit them up and faded. She started forward with her hand out.

"Decianus!"

Behind them as they swung around, following her glance, the door closed, and the old woman's hand fell into her lap. Decianus had gone, and they were alone in the room with a self-confessed murderess, yet the pain in her face was such that Camillus felt only a sick and helpless pity.

"Madam," said Thrasea Paetus, "that was nobly done, a sacrifice in the true spirit of Rome, but you cannot expect—"

"Expect? I expect nothing, I can hope for nothing now." She cut across him. "Yes, I am a Roman and you have shown me my duty. I regret nothing and I hope that you in your turn can say as much. Now let me pass."

She rose and swept toward the door with the authority of an empress. Someone's eye must have been at the crack, for it opened before she reached it and slammed behind her, a moment before the senator's hand could touch her. He turned quickly to Camillus, who had thought more slowly, but then drew back.

"No, not now, she was right. She is a Roman and that gives her certain rights."

"But, sir, where are they going? They'll both escape!" Camillus was crying now.

"Decianus perhaps, for the moment, while I decide what had best be done about him, and while he is prepared to skulk in hiding outside the city. Domina Faustina, no; she has not gone out to escape but to die. Listen!"

Outside there was a wail and the sound of someone hammering on a door. They went into the courtyard. On the far side the steward was pushing helplessly with his shoulder at a door which had clearly been blocked from the other side by something heavy. Domina Livonia, her hair pulled down and her face tear-streaked, was crying in the arms of one of her women. Thrasea Paetus regarded them grimly.

"Yes, I see that they have the sense not to try too hard, not until she has had time to finish her work. Better a dead sacrifice for the honor of the house; it may yet be that a compassionate Caesar can be persuaded to be merciful."

"But you don't think that she really killed Caius Pomponius, do you?" asked Camillus. "What about the man with the brown cloak?"

Thrasea Paetus looked at him, and his face was still as grim as Domina Faustina's had been. "Oh, no, he was real enough; it was clever of him to use the knife that was already there. This case has taught you many things, Camillus, has it not? About what love and fear can do, and how stark and bitter are the bones of Justice beneath the nobility of her appearance. I am more sure than ever now that Caius's death can be laid at Decianus's door, but it is no longer necessary to prove it. Domina Faustina has chosen to bear the weight of murder rather than to live with the knowledge of what her favorite son was capable of. For he has betrayed her a second time and left her to her fate."

"What can we do now?"

Thrasea Paetus took him by the arm and led him out of the house. The front door was open and the porter let them go. Camillus felt the freedom and racket of the streets outside like a return to life from the caverns of the underworld; then he remembered that the house had seemed like that even before he knew the evil secret that it contained.

They stopped at a fountain where the street widened into a small square opposite the temple of Serapis. The senator sat down suddenly on the rim of the stone basin as if he were very weary.

"I suppose that from one point of view we could say we have succeeded beyond our wildest dreams. But we must still use that success, and in such a way that if possible we can rebuild the shattered fortunes of the family of the Pomponii. There has to be an official explanation of the death of Faustina. Decianus can be ignored for the moment. Also we need authority for the release of the slaves."

"Can we go to the praetor?"

"No. Nor would the prefect of the city guard be likely to respond to a plea for mercy and the discreet avoidance of scandal; he has too great a reputation for cruelty. No, we must aim high. I shall seek an urgent interview with the Emperor."

Camillus felt suddenly sick again. It had cost him more than he would admit even to himself to go to the house of the Galli, and now an even darker pit was yawning wide at his feet. What had already happened had left him cold with horror, yet Thrasea Paetus was asking him to face even worse. And surely it would be useless, anyway.

"What can we say that has any chance of success?" he asked bleakly.

"Camillus, I am not going mad. It is no disgrace to kneel in the dirt when one is tending the hurts of a friend. We shall try bribery and flattery. We owe it to the dead, who have thought and acted very much as we might have done in their places. The Emperor is a poet, and I think we can spin a tale out of this misery and confusion to touch his heart. That will be enough."

He stopped and looked hard at Camillus's pale and troubled face. "You should be with me. You are a friend of the dead man's son, and perhaps the only member of the family left with the right to act for them. But it won't be easy; say now if this is an ordeal that you cannot face. Better to admit weakness to me than to crack before the Emperor. I should think none the worse of you."

Camillus saw a way of escape open for one flash before

his eyes; then he remembered Hylas. If one word, if only his presence at the senator's side could save the slaves an hour in prison, then he must go. It no longer seemed strange to him after four days that this was so.

"Give me time to put on my best toga and deal with my wife. In an hour I will be ready."

XV

THE EMPEROR

ANYONE COULD ENTER the outer areas of a palace where thousands of people lived and worked. The courtyards were full of senators, attendants, and hangers-on at almost any hour of the day or night. However, some among them had work to do, because the largest empire the world had ever known needed secretaries to write letters and administrators to pacify ambassadors while the Emperor practiced the lyre or sang his own verses.

Thrasea Paetus stopped in the first presence room and looked about him for someone he knew. It was clear that in spite of the festival the Emperor was not giving a banquet, and that was good.

He fixed his eyes on a man dressed in the Greek fashion in an elaborately embroidered robe. An unlikely acquaintance, Camillus thought, as he watched the man talking to two guardsmen. Still, when the senator caught his eye, he acknowledged the greeting with a show of pleasure and got rid of his other company quickly.

"Tribune, I believe you are not acquainted with Dionysios, Imperial Secretary for Correspondence from the Eastern Provinces," said Thrasea Paetus. "It is fortunate for us that he is a man who delights to be of service to his friends."

Strange for a fat Greek freedman to be the friend of one of the most distinguished members of the Senate, thought

147

Camillus. But before many minutes had passed he had changed his first quick estimate of Dionysios; this man was very clever indeed. The senator had told him only part of the story, but clearly the experienced mind had already filled in most of the gaps.

"I see, yes, you may be right. You can at least do no worse than fail. I think fortune is with you in that it is one of 'Our' literary evenings. An audience may not be possible, but I can try. I hope you are both well acquainted with the works of the Greek poets!"

One word from Dionysios passed them through the next guarded door and into the private labyrinth of the palace. As they followed him down corridors of marble and up steps where they seemed to be jostled by a motionless procession of gods cast in bronze, the senator spoke quietly to Camillus.

"Flattery within reason I can manage, but this sort of foolishness is beyond me. I'm not sure what Dionysios means."

For the first time in the whole difficult day he seemed unsure of himself, his austere manner out of place at the frivolous court. And there was no time to plan together what to do. Camillus had only the rough outline of what had been in Dionysios's mind to go on.

"I think he expects we may need to play some sort of part with the Emperor, like actors pushed onto the stage not knowing what play is being performed. Well, my schooldays are not so long ago. Fortuna grant that I may be quick to catch my cue!"

There was no time for any more, and he did not notice the relief in Thrasea Paetus's eyes. They were on the edge of a bustle of slaves and stewards clearing away what looked like the last course of a dinner. There were lights ahead, clustered on bronze stands, through the doorway of a room pillared in dark-green marble. There was a smell of wine and a suffocating waft of dying violets and bruised leaves, laughter and the notes of a lyre.

"Wait," whispered Dionysios. "I think your arrival may have been well timed."

He went forward alone, and Camillus noticed with interest that he was important enough for the chamberlain who was supervising the clearing away of the meal to leave his duties at once to talk to him. He summoned the captain of the detachment of guard on duty in the area of the imperial dining room.

When he came back, his expression was hopeful. "A message has been sent in," he said. "You are fortunate that Annaeus Seneca is with the Emperor, which is unusual these days when it is an artistic evening. I think Seneca finds them 'difficult.' I have sent in a message requesting an immediate audience for the consular Thrasea Paetus. If it is any help to you, they have been listening to a reading from the *Medea* of Apollonius Rhodius."

They waited then for what seemed a long time, while fresh garlands were carried in and a girl's voice tinkled prettily above the sounds of conversation and laughter. Camillus was racing through the plot of *Medea* in his mind. If it fell to him to speak, an idea was forming. Then the chamberlain appeared in the doorway and signaled to the centurion.

"May Fortuna favor you and grant me to be of service again, gentlemen," said Dionysios, fading discreetly away.

Feeling even worse than he had when he arrived at winter quarters to meet the difficult legate of his first legion, Camillus followed Thrasea Paetus into the room.

It seemed hot and brightly lit after the torches of the corridor. The evening was one for violets: the pillars were garlanded with them and the cushions were covered with purple silk. It was a party of nine; the Emperor, reclining on the central couch in a robe of white silk shot with silver, was in deep conversation with his neighbor. Before them a kneeling slave with gilded curls held the scroll they had been studying.

Seneca, the Emperor's former tutor and chief adviser, was placed on his right hand; he saw them pause in the doorway and signed for them to come forward. He looked thin and ill, out of place among the other company of fashionable authors and expensive noblemen young enough to be his sons, who lounged in their brilliant robes on the other couches.

"Your business is urgent, Senator?" asked Seneca. "The time, as you can see, is not exactly suitable for the serious consideration of important matters."

"I believe our petition is one that will move the heart of the Emperor," said Paetus, aware out of the corner of his eye that Nero was beginning to give them his attention.

Seneca's face delicately showed his disbelief, but he leaned back on his cushions and said, "Caesar, your suppliants are here."

Nero twisted around and sat up to look at the two men. In the pause before he spoke, Camillus, who had never been so close to him before, noticed how the silvered robe showed up his spotty complexion and that from above the fine blond curls were thinner than they had seemed. He looked like a pudgy boy now, but at this rate he would be a fat man by the time he was thirty.

"Gentlemen," he said, "the hours I can spend with the muses are all too short. I trust the urgency of your business justifies this intrusion."

Camillus was standing close enough to Thrasea Paetus to feel the tremor that went through him. For all his talk of flattery outside, now the words stuck in his throat. It was well known in Rome that the Emperor had been displeased more than once by the uncompromising attitude he had taken in the Senate; he had risked much in asking this audience. Without his influence Camillus would never have got so far, but now he must go on alone.

"Noble Caesar," Camillus said, bowing with a disarmingly honest smile, "we have come to you not as citizens to their ruler, but as children come to their father when the misdeeds of the day must be confessed before they can go trustfully to bed."

Before Nero laughed, and Camillus dared to raise his eyes again, he was sure that his heart missed three beats. "So my children have been naughty!" He was only eight years the older of the two. "Whose deeds have you come to confess, your own or another's?"

"Caesar, I am here on behalf of a family who in these last days has been cruelly afflicted by fate. It is a family to which I have been allied by marriage only recently. You will remember the murder of Caius Pomponius Afer, my father-in-law; we pray for your help in saving those who are still living from further suffering, for already his death is casting back a cruel shadow from beyond the grave."

"How? Have there been more deaths?"

"Caesar, on this evening of festival I hesitate to speak of

the dark story of the past days, as we have seen it, the noble senator and I. Only the knowledge that you have already been moved with the story of the strange passions of Medea gives me courage. I wish I had the words of a poet to stir you as deeply."

Suddenly, with the sixth sense he had learned to recognize during his first lessons in schoolboy rhetoric, he knew that he had got his audience. The Emperor was leaning back on his elbow, preparing to be harrowed and appalled. There was to be no chance of a private explanation: the story would have to be shaped into something for a public occasion. Even the slaves had stopped their noiseless padding to and fro behind the couches to hear what he was going to say. Fortuna, Camillus breathed, two silver statues!

He began. He made a twisted story of dark loves out of the small doings of the family of the Pomponii that would not have been out of place among the most terrible of the Greek myths. Faustina became a figure of frustrated and destroying love. Like an artist he laid his paint on thick to cover the faulty drawing beneath. She had been tormented by strange fancies. Under their spell she had killed, she had admitted her guilt, and she had died by her own hand. Her other son was now absent from the city on urgent business connected with his stepbrother's death. The family lay crushed between the double burden of its master's death and its mistress's crime. Only Caesar, like the god who comes at the end of the play to settle everything, could speak the healing words that would cleanse the family from this double sacrifice of blood. Otherwise innocent slaves would be put to the torture, the provisions of wills be set aside, even bequests to the Emperor.

The Emperor's eyes lit up, as Camillus had known they

would, at the mention of a bequest; he was like a child about presents. That word had broken through the highly colored tide of oratory to which he had listened, his face flushed, like a silly woman at the theater.

Camillus ceased, and waited with his head bowed. Paetus put a hand on his arm, but he could not tell if the senator was trembling, too, or if it was only the pounding of his own blood.

"Apollonius, you should be living now! Tribune, you are an artist, for only one who has been found worthy by the gods could be given such a gift to move men!"

Raising his eyes to look the Emperor in the face, Camillus said, "I own no dead man my master while the dead are surpassed by the living. Could it be that some day this dark tragedy might inspire your own art?"

"What do you think, Lucan?" Nero's smile was brilliant as he turned to the very young and handsome man on his left. "Could it be done?"

"And the family of Pomponius Afer, Caesar?" asked Seneca, in an ironic tone that the Emperor did not notice.

Nero turned back regretfully, and when he spoke, it was quietly, so that only Camillus and Thrasea Paetus could hear. "You say there is some matter of a bequest?"

"I understand the known devotion of Caius Pomponius to the imperial house has been worthily expressed," said Thrasea Paetus. Camillus turned his face away until he could still a fatal twitch of his mouth; it would be cheap at the price. Paetus seemed to have recovered himself.

"For tonight your word of comfort would be enough for the stricken family; that and an instruction to the warden of the prison to free the household slaves. In the morning a letter of condolence and of acceptance of the bequest would still any doubt in the public mind as to what has happened, and establish the family beyond the reach of malicious gossip."

"It shall be as you wish." At a sign from the watchful chamberlain a slave with tablets on which the order was written appeared at the Emperor's elbow; that would be Dionysios again! Nero pressed his signet into the wax. Camillus's hand trembled as he took the precious tablets and put them into the fold of his toga.

"Now, Tribune, the father has calmed his children and you have given me an idea for a new poem. Will you not stay and help me begin it?"

"Would you delay the bearer of good news, Caesar? At any other time Camillus Rufus would be overcome with the honor you do him," said Thrasea Paetus smoothly.

Camillus, struck speechless by the thought, clenched his hands inside his toga. He bowed for the last time and felt a hand on his elbow steering him out of the room.

"Dionysios will see to it that the letter is written and signed in the morning," said the senator, when they were the length of a corridor away from the dining room. "Steady, Camillus, you've won, you can't faint now!"

"I'm not going to faint, I'm going to be sick." Camillus disappeared behind a cluster of palm trees growing in terra-cotta pots. When he came back a little later, he was still white around the mouth and his forehead was beaded with sweat; he leaned weakly against the pillar.

"I don't think I could do that again, sir, even if it would save my own life," he said. "If I'd understood what it would be like, I should never have had the courage to come."

"A braver exhibition of bad taste I have never seen," said Thrasea Paetus, looking at the young man with weary approval. "You succeeded where I would have failed utterly. We have placed a terrible burden upon the dead, but I think the living will bless us, and the doing of it must be our sacrifice on the altar of justice. Come now, your friends are waiting."

XVI

SON OF PYLADES

HYLAS WAS LYING on his stomach on the bed in one of the small guest rooms of the Villa Pomponia; he was clean and warm, and when Nissa had finished dressing the wounds on his back, he might be comfortable for the first time in many hours. Meanwhile, he was hanging on to the end of the bedframe and trying not to make too much noise.

It was the second hour after midnight, but there still seemed to be lights in every room in the house. Thrasea Paetus had sent his own steward ahead to make preparations for the care of the slaves of the household, and the senator himself was standing in the middle of the atrium while the last few, who had needed to be carried, were brought in from the wagon outside. The dining room was now a dormitory for men, but Hylas had been put on his own. Clouds of steam were floating from the kitchen, where caldrons of water had been heating for hours; there was a sharp smell of herbs and ointment disguising the stench of prison clothes and sick bodies. The house was beginning to look less like the fringes of a battlefield.

Varro carried a clean bowl of water into Hylas's room and put it down on the table by the bed. "Hang on to me," he said, untwining Hylas's fingers from the bed-frame. "Tell me what happened when the tribune got to the prison."

Hylas dragged his mind free from present pain to the marvels of an hour before. Sometimes in a dream one got stuck in the same horrible thing that went around and around. Now he wanted to go on reliving the time when the door at the top of the prison steps had opened and he had first heard Camillus's voice.

"It was funny seeing the guards move so fast after he gave them an order. He's not a tribune for nothing, and yet his voice sounded strange, almost as if he'd been crying. And yet they say he'd been to the Emperor himself and brought the note for our release to Macrobius sealed with Nero's own seal."

Varro, remembering Camillus's exhausted face, thought that he knew what that had cost.

"We didn't believe it at first," Hylas went on. "Mother cried out, 'Oh, he's come,' and then the other women started wailing. The next thing I knew was Camillus down on his knees beside me. I don't think he actually spoke to me at all before they carried me up the steps."

He felt Varro give him a warning nudge as Nissa drew the cover partway over him; he caught his breath even at the weight of that. Then he heard Camillus's voice saying. "No, wait, let me see."

The young tribune looked down at the oozing grid that the lash had laid across Hylas's back and then rearranged the cover gently. Hylas eased himself carefully over onto his side. Nissa cleared away her things and at a glance from Camillus left the room quietly with Varro. The slave and the senator's son looked at each other; they were both almost beyond weariness and it was difficult to know where to start, but some things needed to be said tonight.

Hylas grinned. "To look at us, my lord, you wouldn't know we were the people who won!"

"But it wasn't really a victory we were after, was it? Only that there shouldn't be an injustice. And look what came of that. Domina Faustina is dead, did you know? No, I don't think she did it, I saw Decianus's face, but she carried the burden of it for him."

"Where is he now?"

"Somewhere outside the city, wondering what's happening. He'll come back later, but I think he'll pay, too, in a different way. It was his crime, even though the knife wasn't actually in his hand."

Hylas looked at the grave face. Camillus couldn't really be thinner after only four days, but he looked older. "And us, my lord?"

Camillus smiled for the first time. "I think we've paid, too, for our small triumph—at least, you already have. I don't think my reckoning is over yet, there's still one thing to do."

It was still there between them, the knowledge that had haunted Hylas ever since he had climbed into the villa on the second night. "You do know now who hid the scroll? I wasn't sure if I'd really heard right in the prison."

"Merope told me. That was brave of her."

"So it was the monkey who started it," said Hylas. "My mother was looking down from the women's gallery and saw it come back to Domina Blandina holding something, and I suppose she couldn't get into the library alone to put it back because I was there."

"Three deaths because of her pet monkey! But I think it

would have happened one way or another without Bland-ina."

Hylas looked away quickly, for what was in Camillus's eyes was a very private emotion. He saw his own left arm with the bandaged wrist lying across the clean bedsheet; prison dirt was still deep under the nails. "I didn't think you could come tonight," he said. "I knew there were still three days, even if the fever didn't overtake us. It wasn't plague, you know, just Macrobius being jumpy."

"When I saw you yesterday morning, I knew that it couldn't take three days," said Camillus wryly. "Still, I don't think your sufferings were quite in vain. Only the sight of them would have been enough to make me face both Domina Faustina and the Emperor on the same day. It cost me something, too, to save you, Hylas, son of Pylades!"

Hylas caught his breath at that. Only free men were called by their father's names, and it had never happened to him before. He wondered how Camillus had known what to say.

Camillus said, "I want to tell you one more thing before you sleep. After the papers have been witnessed tomorrow, you will belong to me. In my mind you are already free, but I think you may find it safer for a while to be my slave, at least till all this has blown over. It could look rather strange otherwise. Oh, Hylas, please don't!"

For the slave had pushed himself up so that the cover was nearly on the floor, and when Nissa came fussing in, Hylas was crying into his hands, looking very young except for the bruises that showed like dark stains on his thin, clean body. Camillus took the hands into his and eased him back onto the bed; then he went out into the courtyard. Perhaps it had not been the moment to tell Hylas, but he did not really regret it. They were both almost too tired for sleep and it would be better to lie awake with good thoughts.

The lights around him blotted out the stars that had shone earlier from a moonless sky. He could only vaguely see the darker shape of the insula looming above. And Hylas had dimmed that, twice. Matidia would be sure to be there on her balcony, she would not have missed watching the comings and goings of the last few hours. He looked up and raised an arm in greeting, but there was too much noise going on for him to know if she answered. He must talk to Varro about what could best be done to help her. The household of the Pomponii owed her a lot.

It was not long before dawn when he reached home. The house was quiet, but a lamp was still burning in his wife's room. That could wait until he had slept. Camillus turned into the small room where he had slept as a boy before he was married. The furniture was still there; he unrolled the mattress onto the bed in the gray light, wrapped his toga around him like an army cloak, and lay down. He would have been glad of that much comfort on the nights around midwinter that he had spent chasing Germans back across the Rhine after they had taken to raiding friendly villages. It would be good to be on his way back north again.

From the sun across the floor it was midmorning when he woke. Timon was hovering in the doorway. Clearly the household had decided it was time for him to get up, although they had let him sleep through the early-morning bustle. He wondered as he washed if there was time to go out for a shave before he faced Blandina, but decided against it; he was clean at least. Later he might meet Galerius at the baths; he would not tell him much, not until it was clearer in his own mind, but it would be good to talk nonsense again and remember that he was a soldier on leave.

Blandina was sitting on the edge of her bed in the dark mourning dress that had been made after the death of her father. She did not look up at him but down at her fingers plaiting restlessly in her lap; he noticed that she had been biting her nails, which was new.

"So you've come home at last," she said. It was hard to tell if she was angry or frightened.

"Yes, I've finished what I had to do. You know what has happened, don't you?"

"Aunt Livonia came. My grandmother killed herself, didn't she, but it isn't true what everyone's saying—that she went mad and murdered my father?"

"No, that part isn't true. I rather think your father was killed by more than one person. Blandina, why didn't you put back the scroll your monkey stole from the library?"

Her head jerked up and she looked him straight in the eyes so that he could see that she wasn't frightened. "That stupid slave was in the way, and I read enough of it to know it was important. I didn't dare leave it just anywhere. I couldn't guess what would happen, could I? I knew enough not to take it out of the house."

Blandina was blushing now. For the first time in their short married life Camillus saw that she was at a loss, uncertain of what he was going to do, and minding what it would be. But he had to be quite sure that she understood the effect of her ill-considered action.

"So you hid it in the family shrine. And at the loss of it your uncle panicked and so your father died: I know that and I was hoping you did."

When he had woken that morning the only thought in his mind had been that he must face Blandina with what she had done and then he need never see her again. Divorce was easy, no one would be surprised if he chose to sever his relationship with the disgraced family of Pomponii. The monkey twittered in the corner of the room and he saw that it was sitting on one of Blandina's marriage chests, already packed for a journey. She saw where he was looking.

"I was waiting for you to come back before I went to my aunt. I know she'll take me in. I can't bear to stay in Rome, and you won't want me here, will you? If you . . . you could write to tell me what you decide to do."

"Do you want me to divorce you, Blandina? Is that what you really want?" Camillus asked her. Now he saw clearly for the first time what her life without the protection of his name would be like. Was this what he really wanted for her? After all, he would be going north again in a few days; he had enough to try to explain to his friend Marcus without telling him that he had divorced his sister. When he was next in Rome would be time enough to see what their future together might be.

Blandina looked up then, twisting the ring on her finger, looking unexpectedly young and defenseless. But she had not answered him and it must come from her so he repeated his question.

"No, Camillus. No, I don't. Please. If only I'd known . . ."

"My dear, we never do. Have you learned that now? I don't expect I'll see you again before you leave, but I'll write."

He turned and walked to the door, feeling lightheaded

and empty. The next months would not be easy for either of them, but he was surprised how relieved he had been by her answer.

"Camillus." He looked back. She raised her hand and let it fall again. Perhaps she had been expecting him to kiss her goodbye, but he did not want to do that again, not yet. As he reached the courtyard below, he remembered Merope, and wondered how she would fare with her mistress now. It would be best to say nothing and leave her to make her own life with Blandina, but she had the look of someone who was usually lucky.

Three days later, Hylas and Camillus stood together under the lichen-stained portico of the small temple of Fortuna. It was a working day in Rome, the one before the city festival, when the court should have met. Behind them an ancient guardian was rearranging the votive offerings before his shrine to show off to the best advantage two handsome silver statues of the goddess.

Hylas was feeling shy. It was the first day that his mother, who for the moment was ruling with a rod of iron those of the household slaves who were left, had let him come out, and his legs felt rather wobbly. Camillus noticed that he looked tired, and led him around to the side, where he had noticed a small courtyard with a few old trees and a stone bench.

"We can sit here."

Hylas hesitated, caught his eye, and sat down almost at the same moment. Even sitting there straight-backed and tidy in the house tunic of his new family, he did not look quite like a slave any more, Camillus decided, watching him closely. After a while the silence grew awkward, and Hylas, glancing across at his new master, realized that of the two he was the less embarrassed.

"What happens now?" he asked, smiling. "You can't take me back to Germany. Your service allowance wouldn't cover the cost of a secretary."

"It hardly pays for my valet! Actually, I was thinking of hiring you out."

Hylas's dark brows met in a bar across his face and the smile went out of his eyes. A slave's perpetual uncertainty before a future that is beyond his control, the emotion he had lived with for so long, stirred again after the hope of the last days.

But Camillus was laughing aloud at the sight of him. "Don't worry, I'm not going to let you out by the hour to some tanner to keep his tallies. I was thinking of much more exalted service. This morning early, before we met, I went to the palace. Dionysios, whom I told you about before, was most gracious. I showed him some specimens of your writing that I had found in Caius's library. He seemed impressed both by your attainments and your initiative. There is a vacancy in his department if the idea appeals to you."

Again, with the swift Greek gesture he had used once before, Hylas knelt to kiss his hand, but when he stood up he did not answer directly. One's wildest dreams and ambitions are too much to accept, all at once, even when they are offered by a friend. There was no secretary in Rome who did not dream in the night of this, the widest gateway to power and security for a former slave.

"Perhaps life with the Pomponii has not been too bad a preparation for the palace! I shall try not to disappoint

Dionysios—or you, my lord. It's not often that I'm lost for words, but now I don't know what to say."

Hylas turned his face away. Camillus gave him a minute to recover and then stood up, too, and looked him up and down. "Very elegant you will look in a long tunic, an important servant of the state. Long before I'm a quaestor you will be in a position to do me favors. I wonder if you should grow a philosopher's beard?"

Hylas used the name to his face for the first time, and found he could say it without stuttering. "Camillus, I thought I was a Stoic, but philosophy has not served me well during the last days. I shall have to talk to Varro. He believes in something that seems to work for him, and because of it he helped to save my life."

"We can discuss it together when I'm home on leave next, and Rome is—well, not calmer, but more ordinary. I shall leave your manumission papers with Dionysios and he can act for you as soon as things seem safe. Whatever you believe by then, I know I shall never have reason to regret taking a former Stoic into my household."

As he spoke it was as if some god, perhaps Fortuna herself, told him indeed that such a day would come, and that he would remember then that he had prophesied truly. He put a hand lightly on Hylas's less damaged shoulder and they went out together into the full sunlight, where the swallows were dipping and flickering their shadows across the paving stones under the clear blue sky of April.

ABOUT THE AUTHOR

MARY RAY has had a passion for ancient history, in her own words, "from the age of six when I started at the deep end with the battle of Marathon, and I have never so far been able to write anything with a modern setting." She writes that since that early time she has never felt any strangeness or distance about what she had learned of the people of Greece and Rome and of earlier civilizations. "I was at home in the period in the way that some people are at home in a place or a country. I started with Roman Britain, because I knew what the places looked like, and for me it is important that the three strands of the actual geographical first-hand knowledge, historical research, and imagination should all be as strong as I can make them." Later, Miss Ray was able to travel extensively to the countries in which her later books were set and in each case makes the reader smell, see and feel what it was like to live in that land.

Born in 1932 in Rugby, England, Mary Ray has had a varied educational and professional life. She attended the College of Arts and Crafts in Birmingham and later trained as a social worker in London and more recently, upon retirement "took a B.A. Hons in Classical Civilisation at the University of Kent and then an M.A. in Church History." She worked in shops, factories, a home for unmarried mothers, in homes for the elderly and finally as a civil servant until her retirement in 1988. Throughout most of this time, in addition to traveling and exercising her creative urge in "making almost anything," she wrote her fourteen books and three plays.

The author's Roman Empire sequence of books, of which *The Ides of April* is second, is considered an important achievement in the field of children's historical fiction. It vividly captures not only the daily realities of Roman life just after the time of Christ, but also the excitement and tension of Christianity in its early days of secret but astounding growth. Each of the five books takes a different place and set of events, beginning in Corinth *(A Tent for the Sun)*, then to Rome *(The Ides of April)*, to Athens *(Sword Sleep)* and Palestine *(Beyond the Desert Gate)*, and ending in Roman Britain *(Rain from the West)*; each book is as different in emotional feel as in the diverse geographical settings. *The Ides of April* is the only story with the added dimension of the classic murder mystery. In all of the books the reader is drawn into the interesting, intertwined relationships as much as into the historical period.

Mary Ray died in 2003.